MINUS MAGIC

Emma Laybourn

Andersen Press • London

First published in 2006 by
Andersen Press Limited,
20 Vauxhall Bridge Road, London SWIV 2SA
www.andersenpress.co.uk

British Library Cataloguing in Publication Data available

ISBN-10: 1 84270 478 8
ISBN-13: 978 1 84270 478 3

Typeset by FiSH Books, Enfield, Middlesex
Printed and bound in Great Britain by Bookmarque Ltd.,
Croydon, Surrey

Chapter 1

The teacher was watching me, all the time.

I studied the twelve little wooden blocks that sat upon the table. Then, with careful fingers, I began to stack them up into a tower. None of their sides was quite flat. As I added the tenth block, the tower wobbled and fell, scattering itself across my lap.

It was a test for a five-year-old. The trouble was, I was eleven. And I'd just failed it.

'Has Ned always been like this?' Although the teacher was watching me, she spoke only to my mother. Her name was Miss Ibbs. She was as thin and prim and pointed as a splinter.

'Yes, always,' said my mother, her low, gentle voice reminding me that it didn't really matter. Only it *did* matter. I began to build the tower again: four, five, six, wobble.

'He's never been able ... there's never been *any* ... ?'

'No, never.' My mother's voice was quite steady. Unlike my tower.

'Not even a hint?'

'Nothing.'

As I placed the tenth block on the tower, it toppled over again. There was no way to get it to balance, without magic. *With* magic, easy peasy. Without it – impossible. I realised that the blocks were made uneven on purpose, and grew angry.

'Actually,' I said, 'I did do magic, once. I remember flying across the back yard when I was three or four. I nearly landed on the cat.' I thought I remembered it quite clearly: the cat's indignant squall, and my own wild giggling.

'Do *you* remember that?' Miss Ibbs asked my mother.

'No.'

'Children don't usually learn to fly before they're five,' said Miss Ibbs.

'Ned's sister was only four when she started.'

'A sister? Is she ... normal?'

'She's fine,' said my mother.

I recalled, with more certainty, the first time I saw my little sister Ellen do magic, three years ago. She made a biscuit float down from the table when my mother wasn't looking. I felt a huge wave of relief that she wasn't like me, that I hadn't somehow tainted her; and then, in its wake, an equally huge wave of jealousy and loneliness.

That was a real memory. The one of me flying wasn't. It was just a fantasy – a wishful dream.

'The rest of the family?' asked Miss Ibbs, her thin, prim voice made important by the echoes from the cold stone walls.

'Can all do magic,' said my mother. Her hand reached under the table to touch mine.

Miss Ibbs rustled her notes. 'Well, of course. You're related to Kelver Truso,' she said with a new note of respect.

'Uncle Kelver,' I said.

'He's not really your uncle,' my mother corrected me mildly. 'He's your second cousin. You only call him uncle because you've known him so long.'

'For ever,' I said, wanting Miss Ibbs to know that Uncle Kelver was as familiar to me as my own parents. Although he lived here in Leodwych City – was on the Mage Council, an important and busy man – Uncle Kelver still arrived periodically back at our little village with pockets bulging with gifts, magic sparkling from his tanned fingertips, and a wide, generous smile that warmed you right through. He brought tools for my father, velvet for my mother, and surprises in boxes for me, wooden dancing frogs and singing bees that I played with constantly until their magic ran down.

'Kelver Truso,' said Miss Ibbs, blushing slightly, 'is a governor of this school. It's thanks to him that we're considering taking on Ned. Normally we wouldn't have the means to admit a child who's so...' She paused.

'Disabled,' said my mother flatly. Under the table, I pulled my hand away.

'That's not a word we use,' Miss Ibbs said with reproof. 'We've had pupils who are – magically challenged, shall we say; a little slow to develop. But I must admit I've never seen a child quite so...'

She glanced sidelong at me. My mother was silent.

'Quite so *special*,' said Miss Ibbs. 'Quite so entirely power free.' She pushed back her chair. 'We'd better go and find the headmaster, Mr Wragg, and let him know you're here. Ned will be in class 4B.'

3

'Then he's in?'

'Oh, yes. Kelver Truso has already paid the first term's fees. Ned can start today. We've arranged lodgings for him in town. You've brought his bags?'

'Yes – but...' My mother looked dazed. She hadn't expected anything so sudden, so soon. Neither had I. I felt a sudden sick panic at the thought of not going home.

Then I reassured myself. Uncle Kelver *wanted* me to come here to Leodwych School. It was ancient and famous, steeped in magic. Surely, if I could learn magic anywhere, it would be here. Kelver had arranged it, so it would be all right.

Miss Ibbs click-clacked ahead of us, heels tapping briskly like little hammers. We walked down chilly corridors with wonkily-leaning walls and occasional holes in the ceiling, which I assumed were water-proofed with spells. She paused under a crumbling archway to let us catch up.

'I expect you find Leodwych a very big place after your farm.' It took me a moment to realise she was actually talking to *me*.

'Oh, yes,' I said politely, although on our way here through the town, it wasn't its size but its higgledy-piggledy confusion that had perplexed me. Leodwych was a mazy tangle of crooked streets, a clatter of hooves and cartwheels, that unexpectedly opened out into quiet, shabby courtyards where grass peeked between the cobbles. It had two bustling markets, a harbour full of shiny new fishing boats with clanking masts, and a fine bridge over the river, which I gazed at with pride, because Uncle Kelver had built it. Not with his hands, but with his magic.

The old bridge was still there too, with deep wheel ruts worn into its stones; and the ancient Guildhall, its broken pillars glued with spells. And, of course, there was the famous Plaza with its fountain and statue of Leode, the First Mage. His face was blurred with age and rain.

If the town really had been planned by Leode, I thought, he hadn't done a very neat job. But of course it was five hundred years old; you couldn't expect neatness.

The same went for the school. Leode built that too, and it was a real scrambled pudding of a place. We followed Miss Ibbs through a hotchpotch of brick and stone and wood all magically patched together. The clock tower leaned over as if it was trying to look through the windows. I hoped the spell holding it on was a good strong one.

Miss Ibbs trit-trotted us to a huge oak door, and turned the handle cautiously. A tide of voices flooded out, followed by a large rock which flew over our heads, crashed into the lintel, and thudded to the floor at my feet.

I peered into the classroom. High, arched windows, rusty shields and axes fixed on the walls – and a whole barrow-load of rocks whizzing like lethal snowballs through the air. My mother quickly uttered a shielding spell.

Beneath the barrage of flying rocks, about thirty pupils lounged at their desks, talking, laughing and eating, as loud and careless as a flock of magpies. My stomach wound itself into an apprehensive knot. There were more children here than in the whole school back home. In their midst was a large man, his red gown flapping frantically as he whirled round like an incensed, scarlet parrot.

'*Put – them – down!*' he roared. All the rocks in front of him descended obediently to the desks. Behind his back, a new set rose up and began to do loop-the-loops.

Miss Ibbs whisked us out and swiftly closed the door. 'We'll introduce Ned later. Perhaps you'd like to see the library? It's upstairs.' She trotted briskly over to a staircase where two boys were sitting, playing dice.

I looked up the stairs – all six of them. A gap yawned to the ceiling, where a lone, broken banister dangled.

'Um,' I said.

'Ned can't get up there,' my mother murmured.

'Oh, he can't fly, can he?' announced Miss Ibbs, too loudly. The boys looked up with sharp curiosity. 'Don't worry, the stairs will be mended. Kelver Truso said he'd pay for all the necessary alterations, as well as Ned's school fees. Now then, Jay? Bruno? What are you doing here?'

'We got sent out by Mr Wragg,' said the shorter boy. His fair hair was spiky and unbrushed. 'For bringing his fossils to life.' He gave a quick, dancing grin.

Miss Ibbs tut-tutted. 'Silly boy, Jay. However, since you're here... You both lodge at Mrs Bolsher's, don't you? I'd like you to take Ned over there. Mrs Bolsher is a very respectable lady in town,' she explained to my mother, 'who looks after several of our boys. Where's his luggage?'

My mother had left my bags with a doorman. While they went to fetch them, I smiled experimentally at Jay and Bruno. Jay half-smiled back. Bruno, heavy-set and ponderous, glared.

'What lesson was that?' I asked.

'Geology.'

'What sort of fossils were they?'

'Ammonites,' said Jay. 'Them big curly ones. I uncurled them and Mr Wragg went mad. You coming to school here?'

'Yes.'

'How do you know Kelver Truso, then?' demanded Bruno.

'He's my uncle. Well, cousin really.'

'Has he found the Necromancers yet?' asked Jay.

That flummoxed me. I didn't know anything about any Necromancers. So I just said, 'I don't think so.'

'Why can't you fly?' said Bruno suspiciously.

'I can't do any magic.' It felt odd, saying it. I'd never said it out loud before. I never had to, back home where everyone knew me.

'Why come here, if you can't do magic?' asked Bruno.

'I'm going to learn.'

'Nice to have a rich uncle,' he grunted.

I kept my mouth shut. I wished Miss Ibbs hadn't mentioned Kelver. I didn't want to be labelled as the useless kid who was only here because of his uncle's money.

My mother returned carrying my meagre bags, and Jay and Bruno led us through the streets to find my lodgings. Bruno was sullen, but Jay answered my mother's questions politely enough.

Yes, he'd been here three years. No, he came from the town, but his parents were dead. Yes, he liked the school fine. Yes, the teachers were – fine. (I sensed some hesitation there.) Yes, the lodgings were fine, and Mrs Bolsher was all right. There was no hesitation, there, at least.

Mrs Bolsher was broad, loud, and breathless. Her lodging-house, tall and narrow, overlooked a cobbled yard. I was to sleep right at the top, in a well-scrubbed attic crammed with bunk beds. There was a cupboard for my things. The house smelt of soap, and my mother was satisfied.

After our goodbyes – too quick, and not private enough – I sat on my bunk and listened to the boys talking. As more strolled in from school, I tried to catch their names: Antony, Rollo and was it Sander? I watched them fishing dice, cards and flyballs from their cupboards to take outside.

Bruno produced a half-made wooden clock. 'That's good,' I said, and he glanced at me resentfully. 'You going to be a clockmaker?'

'Shut up,' said Bruno. He carted his clock out with the others. Through the window, I saw them gathered on the cobbles, chatting and knocking a flyball around. When it got stuck in a gutter, Rollo flew lazily up to roof height to retrieve it.

I thought about joining them. But I didn't want to seem pushy. And of course I couldn't play flyball.

So I lay on my bunk – which was narrow, but not too hard – and let myself, for a few moments, do what I seldom did back home: let myself dream of the day when I would fly too, zooming round the rooftops like a crazy crow; when I would turn water to fire, stone into honey, wasps into dragons; when I could become invisible as easily as sneezing.

Because everything was possible, now.

Chapter 2

When I came down to breakfast next morning, Mrs Bolsher embraced me in a tight, wheezy hug.

'Look at those bleary eyes! Could you not sleep? Poor, homesick lad,' she husked, and then, thankfully, seemed to think she'd done her duty by me and asked no more questions apart from offering extra porridge. So I didn't tell her I would have slept fine if only the bed-clothes hadn't kept tying themselves around me, and if my bed hadn't started doing a jig in the middle of the night. I'd heard muffled laughter, but no one owned up.

No one was speaking to me at breakfast, either, until Jay mumbled, 'Pass the jam.' As I picked up the jar, it yanked itself from my grasp and crashed to the flag-stoned floor.

Mrs Bolsher hurried in from the kitchen. 'What was that?'

'Sorry,' I said. 'It just slipped out of my hand.'

'We don't play with our food in *this* house, Ned. Anyone who wastes good food on magic tricks will find themselves on short rations.'

'Sorry.'

'Clear it up, please.' As she bustled away to fetch a cloth, I got down on my knees and started picking up the bits of sticky glass that seemed to cover the whole floor.

'It'd be easier if you helped,' I said to the feet around me.

'Wasn't me,' said Jay.

'It was *somebody*.'

Nobody answered. Nobody helped, either. Still, no more food got thrown around, so I reckoned it could have been worse.

It got worse.

Trudging a careful distance behind Jay and Bruno, I followed them to school: not to Mr Wragg's classroom, but to another high-arched room whose rickety desks were meticulously carved and inked with names, dates and spells. I slid into a corner chair, and read my desk lid: **CAV WOZ ERE IM BORED**. It was dated thirty years ago.

'Ah! The new boy!' The young teacher bounded over to give me an exercise book and a long, thin box. 'Here you are, Ned. I'm told you need these. *Pencils!* Look after them! They're very expensive.'

I opened the box and fingered the pencils inside. Back home, in Miss Plumbly's class, we'd used slates and chalk.

'Mr Fellows? How come he gets pencils and we don't?' demanded the red-headed girl next to me, her eyes narrowing.

'Hush, Marta!' said Mr Fellows, kind and embarrassed. 'You don't *need* pencils. Come along, everybody! Long division. Start with these examples in your books, please.' He wrote with his finger in the air, leaving big, black numbers wavering like smoke.

A few children bent their heads to their books, dutifully muttering, 'Let it be solved.' The sums appeared on their pages, neatly writing themselves out, answers and all. But most people were watching *me*. I chose a pencil from the box and began to copy down the sums.

'Why don't you do it the normal way?' whispered Marta.

'He can't do magic,' said Bruno behind me. Everyone stared.

'What do you mean, he can't do magic? None at all?'

'Spaz,' sneered a big, grinning boy with no eyebrows. 'Cripple. Necromancers'll get you.'

'Shut up, Gowan,' said Jay.

One of the pencils rose slowly out of the box and began to turn a somersault. I grabbed it and put it back.

'How do you do your sums?' asked Marta disbelievingly.

'I work them out.'

'In your *head*? Without magic? But that's so slow! And don't you get them all wrong?'

'Not always,' I said. As another pencil lifted itself out of the box, I replaced it firmly and put the lid on. Mr Fellows was busy burrowing in a cupboard.

'Do you always use a pencil?'

'We used slates at my old school,' I said, remembering how Miss Plumbly would rap people over the knuckles if she caught them solving maths by magic. 'Work it out *yourself*!' she'd snap. 'Don't be so *lazy*!'

I hadn't stood out like a lemon in a bowl of apples, back there. I'd been different – but not too different.

I felt very different here, scratching away with my

12

expensive pencil. My box was sliding open again and I put my left hand on it to keep it shut.

It opened beneath my hand, and a pencil poked me in the palm. I laid down the one I was writing with to place both hands on the box.

'Give it a rest,' I said.

Two things happened.

The pencil I'd just put down squirted itself into the air and perched behind Jay's ear. And the box I was gripping tightly with both hands lifted off the desk and rose up in the air.

I should have let go. I was stupid. I felt myself being hauled upwards, and didn't let go. I'd played this game with friends back home: they'd lift me up for fun, and fly me around a bit.

But my friends never took me too high, and they always let me down gently. Right now I was heading for the ceiling, which was a long way up. I squinted down at Jay, gazing open-mouthed with my pencil behind his ear.

'Let me down!' I called. Mr Fellows pulled his head out of the cupboard and immediately started shouting.

'Come down at once, boy! You know that flying in class is forbidden!'

Then, with a shock, he realised it was me. 'Don't worry! I'll bring you down!'

I felt his magic tugging at my feet. But someone else was still pulling me up, and I was being stretched in the middle.

'Ow,' I said. I let go of the pencil box and found

13

myself zig-zagging helplessly across the classroom, bouncing like a ping-pong ball between Mr Fellows' magic and someone else's, air-sick and angry.

'*Ow!*' I skimmed the desks, did a cartwheel over Mr Fellows' head, smashed into the blackboard and slithered down the wall. Mr Fellows, red and flustered, helped me up. Then he turned and bellowed at the class.

'I do not expect to see that happen again!'

'Look away next time, then,' muttered Gowan. If Mr Fellows heard that, he ignored it.

'Write out numbers one to twelve!' he barked. 'All of you!'

I tried not to stagger as I walked back to my seat. My pencil box sat neatly on the desk. It was empty.

Jay leaned over and handed me the pencil from behind his ear. 'Not me,' he mouthed.

I didn't know him well enough to believe him. It could have been any of them: Jay, or Bruno, or Gowan, or Marta, or even the silent girl in the corner who was watching me with a faint, superior smile.

'Back to work, Cassie,' Mr Fellows scolded her. 'Quiet, everybody! The next person misbehaving will be sent to Mr Wragg! No, to Miss Lithgoe!'

Whoever Miss Lithgoe was, her name had quite an effect. The classroom hushed. 'Let it be solved,' came the faint murmurs around me, as everyone returned to their sums.

I tried to concentrate. My hand wouldn't keep steady. I wrote, crossed out, wrote again, doggedly.

I heard the door open, and Mr Wragg's surprised voice.

'Well! I'm glad to see everyone so hard at work.' I kept my head down, writing.

'Long division?' said another voice, one I knew. Uncle Kelver!

My heart leapt. I lifted my head, and there he was: tall, strong-faced and handsome, looking much more agreeable than the sour-faced Mr Wragg. He wore his familiar, long travelling coat with many pockets. The wonders I'd seen emerge from those pockets...

The class stood up. Mr Fellows, sidling over to me, muttered, 'You won't mention...just now?' As if he needed to ask. I didn't want to be labelled a snitch on top of everything else. Uncle Kelver strode across to shake my hand.

'How are you, Ned? Settling in all right?'

I nodded, as he smiled around cheerfully. I could see everyone admiring him. Marta's cheeks had gone pink.

'Is he your *father*?' she whispered while Kelver was asking a stuttering Mr Fellows about the lesson.

'Cousin,' I said, wishing – not for the first time – that my father could be more like Kelver. My father was weather-beaten and preoccupied and silent. I wished he would talk to me and show me tricks, like Kelver, instead of just nodding off in his chair every evening. It sometimes gave me an odd feeling to look at Kelver, as if he should have been my father.

'So,' said Uncle Kelver to me, 'got all your sums right, I hope?' He picked up my book, but I knew he wouldn't care, or give me away, if they were all wrong.

He glanced at the empty pencil box and shot me an enquiring look. I shrugged and he laughed. Then he clicked his brown fingers – I wished I could do that, with such casual mastery – and there were all my pencils, lying in my box again as if they'd never flown away.

'I'll just put a wee holding spell on them for you,' said Kelver, flexing his fingers over the box. 'I think you'll find that no one can borrow them now.' He chuckled so affably that nobody could take offence.

'Thanks.'

'Settled in your lodgings?'

'Oh yes.'

'The new stairs all right for you?'

'Oh yes,' I said again, although the staircase to the library that had appeared overnight was alarmingly wobbly. I suspected it was bodged together with a few nails and a careless spell.

'You'll get an excellent education here,' said Kelver, 'won't he, Augustus?'

'Indeed,' agreed Mr Wragg, grinning and nodding vigorously.

'Best in the land,' said Kelver, 'amongst the brightest pupils in the land.' He winked at Jay, who promptly put his hand up.

'Sir? Have you found the Necromancers yet?'

Mr Wragg's eyebrows shot up in furious alarm. 'Quiet, boy!'

But Kelver replied calmly. 'Not yet, Jay. Not yet – but

Chapter 3

The bell rang. At once everyone started to jostle out without waiting for permission from Mr Fellows. Gowan shoved me.

'*He* can't be your cousin,' he growled. 'He's a Mage! So how come you're so thick?'

'Look who's talking,' muttered Jay.

'It *is* odd, though,' said Marta, out in the corridor. 'Kelver Truso's famous for magic. He can do anything! He made the new bridge, *and* the fishing fleet, *and* the winged sheep on the sports field. So why can't he make you do magic, Ned?'

'He's tried,' I said, because Uncle Kelver *had* tried, many times. I remembered him holding my seven-year-old hands in his broad firm ones, frowning deeply as he chanted spell after spell over our kitchen table until my mother said gently,

'Stop, Kelver. It's no use. You'll only exhaust yourself.'

Kelver had sighed, pushing back his thick hair. 'I just wish I could help. I feel responsible for Ned.'

'Why? It's not your fault. It's just one of those things that happens, nobody knows why.'

But I saw Kelver glance sidelong at my father, nodding off in his chair, and instantly I knew what he was thinking. My lack of magic was my father's fault. My we will. You don't need to worry about them.'

'You don't need to even *talk* about them,' hissed Mr Wragg.

I was bemused. What was all this about Necromancers? Necromancers only existed in fairy stories. They were wicked wizards in tales to frighten naughty children, whom they supposedly stole and ate. They weren't *real*. If they were, Kelver would have told me . . .

Kelver put a reassuring hand on my shoulder. 'Just concentrate on your studies,' he advised. 'Make the most of it! The sky's the limit here – as long as you work. Speaking of which, I mustn't keep you from it.' He slipped me a sovereign, unseen, squeezed my shoulder, and nodded at the pleased pupils as he departed. The room seemed darker and emptier once he had left.

wouldn't care, or give me away, if they were all wrong.

He glanced at the empty pencil box and shot me an enquiring look. I shrugged and he laughed. Then he clicked his brown fingers – I wished I could do that, with such casual mastery – and there were all my pencils, lying in my box again as if they'd never flown away.

'I'll just put a wee holding spell on them for you,' said Kelver, flexing his fingers over the box. 'I think you'll find that no one can borrow them now.' He chuckled so affably that nobody could take offence.

'Thanks.'

'Settled in your lodgings?'

'Oh yes.'

'The new stairs all right for you?'

'Oh yes,' I said again, although the staircase to the library that had appeared overnight was alarmingly wobbly. I suspected it was bodged together with a few nails and a careless spell.

'You'll get an excellent education here,' said Kelver, 'won't he, Augustus?'

'Indeed,' agreed Mr Wragg, grinning and nodding vigorously.

'Best in the land,' said Kelver, 'amongst the brightest pupils in the land.' He winked at Jay, who promptly put his hand up.

'Sir? Have you found the Necromancers yet?'

Mr Wragg's eyebrows shot up in furious alarm. 'Quiet, boy!'

But Kelver replied calmly. 'Not yet, Jay. Not yet – but

16

I heard the door open, and Mr Wragg's surprised voice.

'Well! I'm glad to see everyone so hard at work.' I kept my head down, writing.

'Long division?' said another voice, one I knew. Uncle Kelver!

My heart leapt. I lifted my head, and there he was: tall, strong-faced and handsome, looking much more agreeable than the sour-faced Mr Wragg. He wore his familiar, long travelling coat with many pockets. The wonders I'd seen emerge from those pockets...

The class stood up. Mr Fellows, sidling over to me, muttered, 'You won't mention...just now?' As if he needed to ask. I didn't want to be labelled a snitch on top of everything else. Uncle Kelver strode across to shake my hand.

'How are you, Ned? Settling in all right?'

I nodded, as he smiled around cheerfully. I could see everyone admiring him. Marta's cheeks had gone pink.

'Is he your *father*?' she whispered while Kelver was asking a stuttering Mr Fellows about the lesson.

'Cousin,' I said, wishing – not for the first time – that my father could be more like Kelver. My father was weather-beaten and preoccupied and silent. I wished he would talk to me and show me tricks, like Kelver, instead of just nodding off in his chair every evening. It sometimes gave me an odd feeling to look at Kelver, as if he should have been my father.

'So,' said Uncle Kelver to me, 'got all your sums right, I hope?' He picked up my book, but I knew he father had little magic, and what he had, he seldom used. Of his little magic, I had inherited none. Kelver blamed himself because Kelver had wanted to marry my mother. He'd told me so; it was no secret. If she'd only chosen Kelver, I would have been his son, with magic streaming from my fingers. The knowledge was like a cold shower: exhilarating and painful.

But that was when I was seven. I knew now that it wasn't quite so simple. As I trailed behind the others to the next class, I wondered what I would have been like if Kelver were my father. Would I still be *me*?

Would Kelver send his son here, to shiver in a draughty geography classroom and copy down vague maps that got vaguer the further they got from Leodwych, until they petered out in wiggly lines? Would Kelver's son be one of the show-offs juggling the ink bottles behind Miss Purvis's back? He wouldn't be the one getting sprayed with ink, that was for sure.

I mopped up as best I could with my handkerchief, thankful that the bottles hadn't been full. But I wasn't looking forward to lunch. My heart sank like a soggy sandwich when I followed the rampaging crowd into the dining hall, and learnt that lunch was vegetable soup. I couldn't see this lot following Mrs Bolsher's rules.

Sure enough, no sooner had we sat down than the first slice of bread took off and flapped towards the chandelier to shouts of 'Toast!' Everyone wanted toast. But since they didn't want the lumps of carrot and turnip in their soup, the air was soon thick with discarded flying vegetables and flapping bread. Every now and then, there was a shower of charred crumbs as a piece of toast collided with a parsnip or burst into flames.

I couldn't cast a warding spell like the others to keep the food at bay. Soon I was spattered with soup and covered in crusts. Miss Ibbs, who was meant to be in charge, fled from a giant clump of soggy noodles that chased her out of the room. Everyone cheered and yelled; and then suddenly fell silent, as another teacher marched into the hall.

She was as big and ugly as a standing stone. All she did was *look*. At once the soup collapsed messily back into the bowls, and the toast glided in to land.

'Who's that?' I whispered to Jay.

'Miss Lithgoe. Possibly. She makes copies of herself, and you never know which is the real one . . .' His voice tailed away as she turned her gaze on him.

'Thank you, children,' said Miss Lithgoe calmly. 'Yes, Jay, this *is* me, on this occasion. You have four minutes precisely to finish your lunches, clear your plates, wipe down the tables and go. In *silence*.'

For the next four minutes there was no sound but frantic slurping, then a murmur of spells as the plates were stacked and wiping-down cloths set to work on every table. No one spoke above a whisper until they were outside. Then they all began to whoop and shout.

Jay and Bruno galloped over to the playing field to start a game of flyball. The flock of winged sheep grazing quietly on the field launched into the air with bleats of panic at the invasion. I watched the players zooming skywards, showing off their spins and loops as they dived around the confused sheep, who, truth to tell, were not very good at flying. They kept turning upside down, baaing plaintively as they tried to right themselves. Eventually the flock managed to get out of the way and drifted clumsily down to a safer corner of the field.

'Flyball's overrated anyway,' said Marta. 'Why don't you come and talk to me and Hanni and the others?'

The group of girls eyed me curiously. I could sense a hundred tactful questions waiting to be asked. Cassie, tall and stooping, hung apart, studying me with an intense gaze. I shook my head. I didn't want to be questioned or studied.

So I traipsed over to join the sheep, and watched the players overhead punching the big soft flyball from fist to fist. I thought nobody was paying me any attention. I thought wrong. Suddenly, my head grew as cold and heavy as if somebody had clamped a helmet to it – a helmet that moved. And *hissed*.

I froze and listened to the hissing all around my head. Several long shapes writhed downwards and danced before my eyes. They were wiry brown snakes, with shining green eyes that glanced fleetingly into mine as they coiled and uncoiled. Very cautiously, I put my hand to my head. My hair had turned into a bundle of snakes.

Gingerly I plucked at one that was too close to my eyes. To my surprise, it came away easily in my hand, tail and all, with no more sensation than pulling out a hair.

I heard laughter above me. I knew I ought to laugh back. Not easy, when your hair's snakes – it sobers you up. Gowan landed heavily nearby, making the ground vibrate.

'Nice hairdo!' he said, smirking.

'I prefer it short,' I said.

'Get your famous Uncle Kelver to cut it, then. He can do anything, can't he? But I like it the way it is.'

'Do you?'

'Oh, it's lovely,' said Gowan with a sneer.

'All right,' I said, 'You can have it,' and grasping two big handfuls of snakes, I pulled them from my head. It made my scalp tingle. I thrust the wriggling handfuls at Gowan. 'Make a wig with these,' I said.

Gowan recoiled. Hands flapping, he chanted a spell so hurriedly that he tripped over his words and had to try again. The hissing faltered, as the snakes in my hands stiffened and died.

'That's a bit unkind,' I said.

'They're not *real*!' jeered Gowan. The snakes were shrinking, slipping through my fingers, turning back to brown hairs that lay almost invisible on the ground.

'Were they poisonous?'

'How should I know?' Gowan turned abruptly and leapt back into the flyball game.

I walked away, pulling dead snakes from my hair. They were withering fast. I patted my head again. Apart

22

from a couple of little bald patches, it felt normal. Which was more than my heart did: it was thumping wildly.

The cracked bell on top of the crooked tower went clunk, signalling the end of lunchtime. As I climbed the steps to the door, they rippled under my feet, throwing me backwards. No one else fell over. I picked myself up and shrugged it off; but I felt like I had a stone in my stomach instead of soup and bread.

How long was it going to be like this? Was I was going to be tricked and tripped every step of my way? I had to learn magic, and fast. Until then, I had nothing to fight back with. Nothing at all.

Chapter 4

Somehow I got through the rest of the day. I reckoned they'd get tired of it soon: I just had to hang on. Once I knew some magic, things would change. Jay would stop looking embarrassed when I tried to talk to him. Bruno would stop glowering like a mutinous bull. And I'd be able to deal with Gowan's tricks once I knew a few of my own...

So I had high hopes of my first magic lesson with Mr Wragg the next day. The sky was the limit, I reminded myself, as I slipped into an empty desk, hoping not to be noticed.

Some hope! At once the desk lid began to snap like a toothless crocodile. I pushed my chair away, and it turned to jelly beneath me. I sank, wobbling, to the floor.

I kicked the jelly chair aside. There was a ripple of giggles as I fetched a spare chair from the corner, dragged it a safe distance from the gnashing desk and sat down.

The chair immediately swayed up into the air. Before I could jump off, I was floating high above the class, who shrieked with laughter.

'Hey!' I yelled, exasperated. 'Gowan! Put me down!'

'It's not me, though,' snorted Gowan.

'*Bruno!*'

'It's not me either.'

'Whoever it is!'

'It's that chair,' said Cassie. 'It's spellbound.'

'Oh, come on,' said Marta, 'let's get him down before Mr Wragg arrives, or we'll all get detention.' Abruptly the chair lowered me to the floor and tipped me off. I dusted myself down, looking suspiciously at Cassie.

'What do you mean, spellbound?'

'It's had so many spells cast on it, it's programmed. The whole of Year Two practised levitation on that chair,' said Cassie, 'and now it can't stop itself.'

'That never happened at my old school,' I said. Miss Plumbly wouldn't have allowed it.

'Well, you don't do much magic in the country, do you?' grunted Bruno.

'Someone could have told me!'

'We would have, but you didn't want to talk to us,' said Marta, shrugging. Before I could answer, the door crashed open. With an irritated swish of his gown, Mr Wragg marched in.

Mr Wragg was one of those teachers who always look like they'd rather be somewhere else. He shouted impatiently at everyone for quiet, flung a pile of textbooks around the room, and began to rattle off a history of Leode as if he wasn't listening to a word he said and didn't expect anyone else to either. When Gowan began to carve at his desk, I could see Mr Wragg pretending not to notice.

'Open your copies of *First Mage* at chapter two,' he ordered. Nobody did.

Marta put her hand up. 'Sir? You said you'd tell us about the Necromancers.' The room fell extra-quiet, as if everyone was holding their breath.

'Chapter two,' snapped Mr Wragg.

She put her head on one side, sharp and innocent. 'But Sir, is it true they've taken another child?'

Mr Wragg's face seemed to freeze. 'I don't know where you hear such silly rumours.'

'Yes, but Sir, is it *true*?' persisted Marta. The class stared silently at Mr Wragg. I didn't know what to think. What was this all about? Maybe Marta was just trying to wind up Mr Wragg. If so, she was succeeding.

'*Open* your books, *read* chapter two,' he thundered. 'Then answer the questions. *Quietly!*'

'Let it be read,' muttered Bruno, and his book began to read itself aloud in a low, rather pompous male voice, which was soon echoed on all sides. I found chapter two. It was called 'The Building of Leodwych', and reading its plodding paragraphs was like wading through mud. This wasn't what I'd been expecting from a magic lesson.

No wonder Marta wanted to distract Mr Wragg with Necromancers... whatever they were. Why did everyone here take them so seriously? Kelver had never mentioned them to me.

They couldn't be important. After all, Kelver had said we shouldn't worry about them. Nevertheless, I was curious, and swivelled to ask Cassie if she could explain.

She was sitting behind me with her fingers in her ears

and her eyes on the book, her lips moving silently. I realised with surprise that she read without magic, like me. Why?

She wouldn't look up. So turning back to my own book, I flipped through the first two chapters, and checked the index. There was no mention of Necromancers. It was a terribly boring book. Then I noticed the author's name: Augustus Wragg.

I raised my hand. 'Mr Wragg?'

'What?' he snapped.

'Why is there nothing in the book about the time before Leodwych was built?'

'Because the book is about Leode, the first Mage and Leode built Leodwych.'

'But what was here before?'

'Nothing. Farms. People scraping a living off the land. Nothing worth mentioning.'

'What sort of farms? Arable or livestock?' I really wanted to know.

'Good grief, boy, I don't know! There are no records. People in those days didn't go in for writing, not until Leode wrote the *Book of the City*. I don't suppose you've read the *Book of the City*?' He scowled down his nose.

'Yes, I have, Sir.' Thanks to Miss Plumbly.

'Hmph! Then you should be able to answer the set questions with no trouble at all.'

'Sir?'

'*What?*' Mr Wragg was losing patience, but I took a deep breath, and asked it anyway.

'Who are the Necromancers?'

'Are you being impertinent, boy?'

'No, Sir. It's just that I've only heard of them in stories. Are they *real*?' Although I fully expected the rest of the class to laugh, nobody did, least of all Mr Wragg.

His brows drew together. 'The Necromancers, my boy, are a bunch of lawless bandits with whom you need not concern yourself.'

'Then they *are* real?'

'The old stories were based on truth,' he said reluctantly.

'Do they really steal children?' I persisted.

'Don't be ridiculous!'

'Four this year from the town,' muttered Jay.

'I heard six,' said someone else.

'If beggar children decide to go missing from their miserable homes,' cried Mr Wragg, raising his voice, 'one can hardly blame them!'

'Not just beggars,' said Jay.

'The Council are dealing with it! They will hunt the Necromancers down and expel them from our lands. I will have no more talk of them here.'

'But, Sir—'

'No more questions!' He was working himself into a fine old froth. So I decided to shelve my questions for now, got out my rare and expensive pencils and began to write.

Whether because of Uncle Kelver's spell or Mr Wragg's irritable presence, nobody interfered with me.

Everyone else was letting magic do the work; I could see Marta's page slowly filling with neat, loopy handwriting, whilst she folded a paper tiger and made it dance on her desk. Jay was doing tricks with tiny, thumbnail fireworks, and Gowan appeared to be asleep.

Only Cassie did her own writing. She had a pencil too – a tiny stub hidden in her hand. I took one from my box and offered it to her, but she shook her head.

'Why don't you use magic?' I whispered.

She just shook her head again, distantly. She seemed withdrawn from the rest of the class. They, in turn, left a space around her: not from dislike, I thought – everyone was polite to her – but almost as if they were *afraid* . . .

I was probably imagining it. Anyway, it wasn't my problem. I had a big enough problem of my own – and another question to ask Mr Wragg: the most important question of all. I waited till the end, when everyone was leaving.

'Sir?' I said quietly. 'When will the proper magic lessons start – I mean the lessons on how to do spells?'

'Spells and charms on Wednesdays and Fridays,' said Mr Wragg shortly. He wanted to be gone too.

'How long – I mean, will I be able – I mean, how long will it take me to learn magic?' I waited tensely for the reply.

'That depends,' said Mr Wragg. 'Your uncle's sending a couple of Mages over to assess you. Come to my office after school.'

'Oh! Right! Thank you, Sir.' My spirits lifted. I felt a

whole lot happier, knowing that Uncle Kelver was sorting things out.

That reassurance carried me through lunch and a barrage of fish cakes: it warmed me through a P.E. lesson spent mooching amongst the sheep, kicking the spare flyball around while the game went on above me. It even let me smile when, on getting dressed back in the changing room, I found that my sleeves stretched down to my knees and my trouser legs were twice their usual length, folding in great rolls around my feet.

I spoke to the room. 'Yeah, nice style, but the thing is, I've got to go and see Mr Wragg now. *I* don't know who's playing games with my clothes, and I don't much care – but *he* might.'

No answer. So I shrugged and waddled off clutching at my waistband. By the time I reached Mr Wragg's study, my clothes had shrunk back to almost their right size. I smoothed them down nervously, took a deep breath and knocked on the door.

'Come in,' called Mr Wragg. I paused on the threshold to stare. It was a real wizard's room: shelves bowing under the weight of ancient books, a table crammed with flagons and crucibles, a sooty fireplace filled by an oversized cauldron. A whiff of brimstone hung in the air. Mr Wragg took his magic seriously.

'Sit down, boy. What are you dawdling for? This gentleman and lady have come specially to see you, and their time is precious.'

An old man with a pale blue gaze was eyeing me

doubtfully, so that I felt a bumpkin in my still too-baggy clothes. In Mr Wragg's chair sat an old lady, her face so lined with wrinkles that it looked like a spider's web. They both wore the dark blue robes of the Mage Council. I bowed.

'Sit down, Ned,' said the lady, her voice distant and breathy. A spider's voice. I sat, and she took my hand in her creased one and began to question me. Where had I gone to school before? What did I know of magic? What magic could my parents do? (That was a hard one to answer where my father was concerned.) What magic had I ever done? (None, of course, apart from my dream of flying.)

She scrutinised my hand, stared at my forehead with a cloudy gaze, and finally, slowly shook her head.

'See what you think, Harlo,' she said. The elderly man began to harrumph gruff spells over me, moving his hands up and down my sides as if he were patting invisible cushions. It made me want to laugh. I was so intent on keeping a straight face that when he suddenly said, 'I can divine nothing there at all,' I hardly paid attention.

'What, *nothing?*' said Mr Wragg with a tinge of disgust.

'Not a trace. Do you agree, Dorea?'

'He is totally empty of magic. Clean as a scoured pan,' she breathed. 'Poor boy.'

'Oh, yes,' said Mr Wragg. 'Indeed. Poor boy.'

'Kelver must have known that,' remarked Harlo.

31

'Oh, I'm sure he did, but perhaps didn't want to believe it.' The old woman grasped my hand again and shook it. 'I know that Kelver Truso has tried to give you magic, Ned, but you must not blame his failure. There is no seed of magic within you to grow, you see, and it cannot be planted there.'

I didn't want to understand. 'But I can be taught it,' I said.

'No. There is nothing to work with.'

'But that's what I'm here for, to be taught magic!' I cried.

'No. You may be taught many other things here, but not magic.'

'But that's why Uncle Kelver...' I swallowed. Uncle Kelver had never said it, not in so many words. I had just assumed it. But he had promised me nothing. 'I'll never be able to do magic? None at all?'

'No. I'm sorry, Ned. I'm sure you will develop other talents.' She dropped my hand and stood up stiffly. 'Well, Mr Wragg, thank you for your hospitality, but we must be going. The Council awaits.' Harlo took her arm and they shuffled out together.

I stared at the empty chair. Was that it? Had I been tested, failed and written off for good in that quarter of an hour?

'Well, off you go, boy,' said Mr Wragg uncomfortably. He wanted to be rid of me.

'Sir? If I can't do magic – does that mean I can't stay on here?'

'You can stay for as long as Kelver Truso pays. And he's already paid a term in advance.' He placed an awkward hand on my shoulder. 'Don't worry, boy, we won't throw you out.'

Actually, that was the last thing I wanted to hear. I wanted to be thrown out. What was the point in staying? I wanted to go home.

Chapter 5

Instead, I had to go back to Mrs Bolsher's.

I found Jay and Bruno perched on the empty horse trough in the courtyard, Bruno with his clock on his knee, Jay with a big black case at his feet. Marta was kneeling on the cobbles to do everyone's homework, muttering spells over the books spread before her. Essays scrawled themselves in identical sentences in every book. Her friend Hanni sat nearby on a black case like Jay's.

'What did Wragg want, then?' said Bruno, fiddling with a screwdriver.

'Nothing.' I felt totally empty; scooped out. Scoured, like the old lady had said.

'You all right?' asked Jay.

'Fine.' I started to go inside, but Jay stopped me. 'Bolsher's cleaning. Won't let us in till teatime.' I sat on the cobbles and stared at my knees.

'Come on, Jay,' said Hanni with a sigh. 'Let's get this over with.'

Groaning, Jay reached down to his black case, undid the clasps, and raised the lid. Inside, on a bed of blue velvet, lay a brass trumpet: a double trumpet, with two horns but only one mouthpiece.

As Jay lifted it up, it began to unwind itself. He wrapped his arms round its squirming coils, took a huge

34

breath and blew into the mouthpiece, cheeks bulging. A
tuneless honking noise came out, as the weird instrument writhed vigorously in his arms. Jay grappled with
it and honked some more, getting red in the face. It
wasn't so much a music practice as a wrestling match.
Marta covered her ears, wincing. I didn't: the noise
sounded like I felt. Clumsy and meaningless.

'What *is* that?' I asked when he paused.

'Goosehorn,' panted Jay. 'Stupid thing, get off!' One
of the twin horns was curling around his neck. He
whacked it back into place and managed three more
notes before it tied itself round his arm. Hanni wasn't
doing much better. She had to sit on hers while she tried
to play. It sounded terrible.

'I've heard of goosehorns,' I said. 'Leode wrote about
them, didn't he?'

'Leode invented the damn things,' gasped Jay. 'Stop
it! *Burana men dehi!*' The spell had no effect. If anything, the goosehorn twisted more than ever.

Bruno laughed and balanced his clock on the horse
trough. 'Give it here! I'll sort it out.' Jay untangled
himself from the goosehorn and thrust it at him.

'You can *try*,' he said.

'Now then,' Bruno told the goosehorn, sternly
wagging his finger, 'you listen to me.' He flexed his
broad hands until magic flared from them in a crackling
aura. The goosehorn whipped itself out of his grasp,
reared back with both trumpets and hit him smartly on
the head, twice.

35

Bruno dropped it, yelping. It coiled around his ankle and tried to trip him up.

'Careful!' cried Jay. 'It's hundreds of years old! Miss Lithgoe'll kill me if it gets broken!'

'You can *keep* it,' growled Bruno. He glared at me. 'What are you laughing at?'

'I wasn't laughing.'

'Think you could do better?'

'For goodness sake!' cried Marta. 'I don't know why Leode ever invented those terrible things. Leave it, Bruno. Not worth worrying about. Here, have a toffee.' Pulling out a paper bag, she threw pieces of toffee to all of us.

I caught mine and put it in my mouth. As soon as it hit my tongue, it turned into a pebble. I spat it out and flung it at Bruno. He ducked; the stone toffee hit his clock and the clock toppled backwards into the empty horse trough with a splintering crash.

'You broke my clock!' roared Bruno in anguish.

'You tried to break my teeth!' I yelled back.

'You *laughed* at me!'

I bit my lip to stop myself retorting. If I had to stay on at school, I couldn't afford enemies. 'Sorry,' I muttered. 'I didn't mean to hit your clock. I'll help you fix it.'

'Fix it? *You* can't fix it! It's got real *gears*!' howled Bruno. 'They took me *hours*!'

'He *carved* them,' added Jay, shaking his head incredulously.

I picked the clock out of the horse trough. Its back

panel was broken, and I could see the cogs inside, still turning. It was a nice piece of kit.

'Don't worry, Bru, it just needs a bit of magic,' said Jay.

'You know I'm no good at mending spells!' grumbled Bruno.

'You could glue it,' I suggested.

'*Glue* it?'

'Sure. Can you make glue? You just need flour, salt, gelatine—'

'I can't use *glue* on it! Shut up! Don't touch it! Put it down!'

I retreated and sat down next to the discarded goose-horn. Bruno and Jay fussed over the clock, discussing spells. The goosehorn was spattered with mud, so I wiped it clean with my sleeve. Then, since it didn't attack me, I lifted it gingerly to put it in its case. Just trying to be helpful. I expected it to lunge at me, but it was lifeless.

I examined it carefully, working out how to hold it, and found the stops for each finger to press. Then I blew experimentally into the mouthpiece.

'Bronk,' said the goosehorn mournfully, like a dying duck.

'Hey!' yelled Jay. 'That's mine!'

'You're not allowed to play it,' said Marta primly.

'You have to be specially chosen to play it,' said Hanni.

'You have to be *normal* to play it,' growled Bruno. Jay grabbed the goosehorn, which immediately began to squirm. He jammed it into the black case and slammed the lid shut. When he looked up, his face was flushed and furious.

'Leave it alone!' he said.

I got up and walked out of the courtyard. I walked through the narrow, noisy streets of Leodwych for an hour or so, not caring where I went. I was thoroughly lost when I unexpectedly found myself at Leode's old bridge.

I crossed halfway and stared down at the river. It was sluggish and sleepy, nothing like the bright ribbons of streams that leapt down the hills back home. Upriver, Kelver's gleaming new bridge spanned the water in a graceful arc. It was a dazzling piece of magic, as perfect as a rainbow. I gazed on its immaculate, shining curves until the Guildhall bell chimed six.

Reluctantly I began to trudge back to Mrs Bolsher's. Where else could I go? I couldn't go home. I wasn't even sure which way home *was* from here...

Surely, though, I could find out. It wouldn't be that hard. Although it felt a thousand miles away, home wasn't really all that far...

It was on the long walk back that I started planning how to run away.

Chapter 6

I knew I wouldn't really do it. It would have meant giving in, and disappointing Uncle Kelver. My plan was just something to hold onto when my books changed into bricks and my pencils into giant maggots, when my desk burst into green flames and Mr Wragg was more annoyed about the scorched desktop than my singed hair.

Through it all I kept saying to myself, I can always run away. In the dining hall, doggedly stuffing myself before the bread could turn mouldy or the beans into tadpoles, I plotted my escape.

Not in the middle of the night. I couldn't creep out of my bunk unnoticed. Not during school: the teachers would ask questions, even if the children didn't. The best time would be straight after school, when nobody would care where I went – least of all Jay and Bruno. I had stopped following them around after Bruno offered me a lift on a flying rug and it shook me off over a puddle. Jay had laughed. He hadn't forgiven me for taming his goosehorn.

They'd just shrug if Mrs Bolsher asked where I was. She wouldn't worry until bedtime: that'd give me hours to get away.

I began to hoard biscuits and apples under the clothes in my cupboard. I spent lunchtimes in the library, studying maps, memorising my route through the town towards my home.

Home. I couldn't help thinking about it, more and more. Memories of home stole up and ambushed me. I couldn't help missing my mother, and my lost friends, and even my dour father; and Uncle Kelver, who had not been able to visit me since that first day. He sent me a letter full of his travels, and enclosing a sovereign. It didn't mention my failure at magic. Maybe he hadn't heard from the Mages: maybe he was being kind in not bringing it up. I treasured the letter, and kept his sovereign safe.

With my secret plans as armour, I endured another three weeks at school. I did sums and wrote essays – with a giant maggot when necessary – and found that if I didn't talk to people, after a while they didn't talk to me. I survived in silence until the day the gymnasium floor turned to treacle.

I still don't know who did it, and I expect it was done to annoy Mr Wragg, not me. But, of course, I was the only pupil who couldn't float across the treacle floor. I had to wade through and leave a trail of sticky black footprints all the way down the corridor.

'Clean all those up *now*, boy! You should have gone *round*!' boomed Mr Wragg. He knew as well as I did that there was no way round, and one drop of his magic could have cleaned the footprints a hundred times faster than my bucket and brush. I spent the afternoon scrubbing down the treacly corridor, and then I ran away.

It was just as well I'd planned it beforehand, because I couldn't think straight. My brain switched off and let my feet make the decision on their own. They didn't bother taking me to Mrs Bolsher's to collect my clothes and hoarded apples. They carried me straight along the route that was reciting itself inside my head: 'Second left, across the Plaza, right at Leode Way...'

I walked, head down, past all the famous sights. All I saw of the Plaza was its broken mosaic floor. In a quiet street past the Guildhall, I turned my blue school cape inside out. It wasn't quite a cloak of invisibility, but it was halfway there, being dull grey on the inside. I used a sovereign to buy one pasty for my stomach and two more for my pockets, drank from a street fountain, and kept walking until I reached the edge of town.

There, lined by a straggle of houses, lay the long west road, wide and dusty, stretching out to the hills over twenty miles away. Once I had passed the houses, I cut across the meadows. I knew my way home now without the road. All I had to do was follow the beckoning sun.

Tramping through the fields, meeting only indifferent cows, I gradually began to feel more myself. The sun slid down with a last cheerful wink; the sky blushed, then darkened, and grew a rash of stars. There was no moon to light the way, so after I'd stumbled into a ditch and bumped into a cow, I decided I'd better stop for the night.

After munching a cold pasty, I wrapped myself in my cloak and lay in the shelter of a wall to gaze up at the stars.

I felt at home here, in the fields. Magic didn't matter here. Animals couldn't do magic, and farmers tended not to use it much. Magic doesn't work too well on a farm. You can't make the wheat grow by magic without it collapsing a week later, and you can't make the rain fall – not more than a little sprinkle, anyway. You can't use magic to milk the cows or shear the sheep. Well, you can, but they don't like it. It frightens the sheep, and makes the cows moody, and the milk yields drop.

The country was where I belonged. At least I could be useful on the farm. I felt guilty about the fees Uncle Kelver had paid to get me into school. I hoped they would give him some of his money back.

As I lay staring upwards, musing on all this, I became aware that something odd was happening above me. In quite an orderly fashion, the stars were going out. A few minutes later, they came on again.

Something was passing in front of them. Not a cloud, for the edges were too sharp. Something big: a long, narrow shape that I couldn't see except by the absence of stars, as if it wore a huge shield of invisibility. It was obviously magical.

Although I had no idea what it was, I resented it. I hated its power, its ability to fly, its invisibility, when I could have none of these things.

It moved away north and I closed my eyes. I must have fallen into a deep sleep, because when I was awoken it felt like being hauled up from the bottom of the sea, groggy and gasping.

A black shadow loomed above me, blocking out the stars for the second time that night; but this shadow was close, and it was *breathing*.

I staggered to my feet, ready to run, when a white light flared out, blinding me. I felt steadying hands rest on my shoulders, and my eyes recovered enough to recognise who stood in front of me.

'Uncle Kelver! I thought you were that thing in the sky,' I blurted out.

'What thing, Ned?'

'That long shadow over the stars.'

He shook his head. 'You were dreaming, Ned. I'm glad I've found you.' His hands tightened on my shoulders. 'You had me worried. I've been hunting all night, since Mrs Bolsher sent a message to say you'd gone missing.'

'How did you find me?'

He held something up in the torch-light: one of my pencils. 'I used a tracking spell. Where are you going, Ned?'

'Home.' I was surprised I needed to tell him.

'Why?'

'Because I'll never be able to do magic. The Mages said so. There's no point me staying at school.'

'Oh, Ned.' He sighed. 'I was afraid of that. But magic wasn't the only reason I sent you there – I wanted to give you a better education than you'd have back home.'

'But I don't fit in.'

'What makes you say that?'

I hesitated. Did he really not know? Could he not guess? 'I just don't.'

He laid his torch on the grass. 'Sit down, Ned.' I squatted and tried to warm my hands at the white flare of the torch, but it burnt with a cold, steady light, with none of the warmth and flicker of a real flame. 'Tell me,' said Uncle Kelver.

So I told him. Sort of. Some of it just sounded too stupid to tell: like the bug-eyed creatures swimming in the water jug, or my shoes turning into lobsters. The shoes would actually have been quite funny, if I hadn't been wearing them at the time.

After a while, I decided it sounded as if I was whinge-ing, so I shut up. It felt good just to sit there in the dark with him next to me. I didn't want to spoil it by moaning about school.

'That shouldn't have happened,' said Uncle Kelver at last. 'None of that should have happened. I feel responsible.'

'Why? It's not your fault.'

'It's because of me you're at the school.' He sighed again, deeply. 'I admit, I did hope that it might help you find your magic.'

'I don't think anything can help,' I said. 'Thank you for sending me there, but I'll be better off at home.'

'You won't go back to Leodwych?'

'No.'

'All right. I'll take you home, for now. It's starting to get light.' He stood up, his tired face grey in the coming

44

dawn, and pulled me to my feet. 'I flew here, but I don't suppose you feel like flying?' I'd told him about being hurtled round the classroom. 'We'll walk,' he said.

It took us till after midday. He commandeered an old barn door and I consented to be flown on that for the last few miles. It felt safer than a carpet.

We landed in the farmyard. My mother ran out of the house and hugged me tight, calling to my father, who came to the door with his lunchtime hunk of bread in his hand. The three sheepdogs bounded expectantly to his feet. My father looked me up and down thoughtfully.

'School not suit you then?'

'Not much.'

'All right. Plenty to do here. Things aren't too good. Some thief stole the hams from the smoking shed yesterday, so we'll have to kill a pig and start again. We're shearing this week, there's walls want mending, and a mountain of wood out the back to be chopped.'

'Sit down and some food first,' cried my mother, bustling us inside.

My father allowed that. He left for the fields with the eager dogs while my mother fed us bread and crumbly cheese and pickles, and plied me with anxious questions. I didn't tell her as much as I'd told Kelver. He covered up for me.

'Ned felt like a break, Mirian. I've sorted it out with the school. But how are you? How are things here?'

'We're doing fine,' said my mother, a little defiantly. Gazing round my home, I thought how small it seemed after Mrs Bolsher's house: how low the ceilings were, and how plain the rooms, compared to Leodwych School. My mother's dress was drab and threadbare.

It seemed Kelver was thinking the same thing. For while my mother was telling us about the calves – her hands busy shelling peas, for my mother's hands were always busy – all of a sudden her grey woollen dress changed to sky-blue silk.

My mother looked down in bewilderment, then laughed. 'Give over, Kelver.'

At once her dress was rags and tatters. 'Is that what you prefer?' he asked, and laughed as well.

'It's all I can afford,' said my mother lightly, 'since our hams were stolen.'

Kelver turned grave and shook his head. 'That's bad. Here, buy some more.' Gold sovereigns tumbled onto the table.

My mother pushed them back. 'Thank you, Kelver,' she said gently, 'but we'll cope. Now, how about my clothes?'

Kelver smiled ruefully, and returned her to her washed-out wool. I got up and went outside, feeling uncomfortable.

I began to chop the wood, a job whose heavy rhythm soothed my nerves. I'm good with an axe, since it takes no magic but merely practice to use one well. Axes and magic don't mix. Magic axes have a reputation for cutting off things you'd rather not, like legs.

As I swung the axe, I tried pretending that the wood

46

was Gowan's flyball or the chomping desk. Then I forgot to pretend and just concentrated on getting my swing right. When I paused, sweating, to rest on the axe, I saw my father watching me with his considering gaze.

'That'll do,' he said. 'You can help me round up the sheep in the top field.'

So we trudged up the hill with the dogs, who herded the sheep to my father's whistles just like magic. They're good dogs: one young and bouncy, one middle-aged and steady, one wise old one ready to retire. He always has the three. All went fine until we reached the sheepfold, and the gate stuck. My father tugged it and wrenched it, but the wood had warped immovably.

My father swore a spell. I heard him spell so seldom that it gave me quite a shock. So did the result: the gate burst explosively off its hinges and rocketed over the wall. The sheep bolted in such a panic that it took us twenty minutes to round them up again.

My father fetched the bits of gate and stood them up against the gap, grunted a mending spell at them, then shook his head. Although the gate was mended after a fashion, it looked and felt flimsy. We left the dogs guarding the flock while we returned to the farm to fetch some wood and tools. My father could have just flown them out, but that wasn't his way.

'That's the trouble with magic,' he grunted as we hammered the nails in. 'Always breaks better than it makes. Breaking's easy. Making's not.'

'It got a bit out of hand there,' I said. It was the sort

of remark they made at school, when a wayward spell shattered a window or flooded the cloakrooms with vinegar.

But my father answered, 'Rubbish. I *let* it get out of hand, because I lost my temper. My own fault. You'd still rather be here, would you?'

'Yes.'

He smiled dryly. 'We'll see.'

He worked me hard all week. I thought he was trying to exhaust me. Once the sheep were shorn, there were walls to mend, potatoes to lift, and sheds to be cleaned out and whitewashed. After Uncle Kelver left, we both sat in silence every evening, nodding over our food. I was too tired even to play with Ellen.

'Still rather be here, would you?' asked my father at the end of each day.

'Yes,' I said.

'Why?' he asked at the end of the week.

'I'll never be able to do magic.'

'You knew that already.' He was right: I *had* known it, until I went to school and got my hopes up. But it was too hard to explain about school to my father.

'I like it at home,' I said. 'I know what I'm doing.'

'Aye. You're handy. But you're not learning owt new.'

'I am!' I cried. 'I'm learning things all the time! I learned about foot rot only yesterday!'

'Aye. But you already know most of what you need to know for here. There's nowt else. There's sheep and pigs and potatoes, and summer and winter. That's it.'

'That's enough,' I said. 'I weren't learning owt at school neither, except how to write with maggots and what to do when my hair is snakes.'

'Useful skills,' said my father. 'This world being as it is.'

'And me being as I am?'

He nodded.

'You want me to go back?'

He shook his head. 'Up to you.'

So I asked my mother. But she, busy mending socks with nifty fingers, not magic, simply said, 'It's your decision, Ned.'

'Think about it,' said my father.

I thought about it. Two days later, I went back to school.

Chapter 7

They crowded around me in the dining hall, eager and curious. For once, my soup didn't spurt into the air; they were too busy asking questions.

'What *happened* to you?'

'Where did you *go*?'

'Did you get *kidnapped*? Did the Necromancers get you?'

'I ran away,' I said. Nobody asked why. They all knew.

'Mr Wragg did his nut,' said Jay. 'He thought the Necromancers had got you for sure, especially after they found the missing kid.'

'What? Was he hurt?'

'Broken leg. He's lost his memory, but they reckon he escaped from the Necromancers.'

'Well, *I* didn't,' I said. 'What would Necromancers want me for?'

'To *eat*,' said Marta. 'To suck your blood.'

'How come they didn't suck that other boy's blood?'

'Because he *escaped*,' said Marta patiently. I didn't believe a word of it.

Half the school remained convinced that I'd escaped from the Necromancers. Those who knew better seemed quite impressed that I'd run away for a whole week. I began to talk again; and they talked back, and played fewer tricks. Gowan still laid stink-spells on my books and shrink-spells on my clothes, but he was the only one – and I realised now that he did it to everybody, not just me.

I realised something else too, on the way into the science room when the door shot open unexpectedly and walloped me in the face.

'Ouch!' I glared around for the culprit, but Jay said, 'That door's just spellbound. So many people have opened it by magic, it does it by itself.'

'It didn't wallop *you*!'

'I lay a counter-spell whenever I go through it. We all do.' Jay shrugged. 'It's second nature. There are so many spellbound things in this place we're doing counter-spells all the time.'

I thought about this. 'The chomping desk?'

'Yep, that's one.'

'The changing-room showers?'

'Sure. And those lamps that keep blowing themselves out – oh, and have any of the dictionaries bitten your fingers yet? They will.'

I hadn't understood that, half the time, the school itself was booby-trapping me. The frenzied forks that stabbed my hands in the dining hall were just suffering the side-effects of too many spells: the flying bread-baskets were spellbound, while the water jugs had grown their very own side effects, small and green with many legs. It was nothing personal. It was just that nobody had bothered to tell me. But now Jay started warning me about the school's hidden pitfalls, and I got better at avoiding them.

51

Not every time, though. A week later, we were in Mr Wragg's room for history. Carefully avoiding the chomping desk, I totally forgot about the spellbound chair, which I sat on.

'Watch—' began Jay, but the chair was already rocketing upwards. I quickly tipped off, skinning both knees, and felt so annoyed at being caught out that I pulled an ornamental axe from the wall and was waiting for the chair when it landed.

'You can't do *that*!' cried Marta, scandalised – but I did. I chopped that chair up into little pieces. Soon the whole class was cheering me on, even Gowan.

Unfortunately Mr Wragg arrived just in time to see the last leg get the chop. He was furious. His eyes bulged; his face turned as red as his gown. The axe was whisked out of my hands and back onto the wall.

'How *dare* you treat school property like that?' he thundered. 'Put that chair back together right now! When I return in three minutes I expect to see it *mended*, and *properly*, or you'll get the beating of your life!' With that he strode out, leaving the class subdued.

'That's not fair,' murmured Marta. 'He knows you can't mend it!'

'That's why he said it.'

'Don't worry,' said Jay. 'We'll sort it. Won't we, Bru?'

'I suppose,' Bruno said reluctantly. He didn't like the way Jay and I were becoming friends. But so many people pitched in to help with the mending spell that two minutes later the chair was back in one piece; and a rickety bodge of a job it looked too. I was reminded of my father's gate.

'It looks like it's going to be the beating,' I said wryly. The class shook their heads in sympathy, which made me feel a bit better about what was coming. I'd never been beaten; Miss Plumbly hadn't believed in it. I wondered if Mr Wragg used a magic cane.

'Wait,' said Cassie suddenly. 'I'll swap it for a spare chair in the attic.' Everyone looked at her in surprise.

'You can't,' said Marta. 'There isn't time. You've got to find one in the attic first, and then how are you going to transpose it through all those ceilings...?' Her voice trailed away, as the rickety chair flickered and vanished, to be instantly replaced by another. It was the same design, just a bit more ink-stained.

'How did you do that?' gasped Marta, amazed.

Cassie shrugged. 'Just did. But he's going to beat you anyway.'

'How do you know?' I asked. The chair looked fine to me.

'Just do.' She bent over her book, and turned a page. Her hands were shaking.

She was right. Mr Wragg hit me on the legs with a cane, for vandalism, he said. It wasn't nice. But after that, I seemed to be accepted.

That was when I first realised there was something special about Cassie. I began to take more notice of her. I saw how seldom she smiled, and how often she rested her head on her hand. People tiptoed around her, giving

53

her tentative pats on the shoulder, then left her alone – almost as if she were a fierce beast that they needed to placate. Yet there was nothing fierce about Cassie.

I followed their example, and left her alone too. I knocked around with Jay and Bruno. Jay was impulsive and funny and always hungry, given to turning his homework into sandwiches and eating it. He couldn't help doing spells. They just leapt from his fingers, so that he frequently left trails of blue bubbles, or puzzled grasshoppers.

I liked Jay, and I tried to like Bruno because Jay did. I saw that Bruno was jealous, and felt himself to be slow and stupid, although he was neither. He was remarkably deft with his big hands, even without the help of magic. Gradually Bruno became less wary of me – almost a friend. Several of the class became almost-friends: they could never quite be real friends, because of my lack of magic, but things were a whole lot better than before.

Lessons were still hard for me. I was struggling with my sums an hour after the others had spelled them out and gone to play. Playtimes weren't so bad, though. I invented a game called football where you just kicked the spare flyball around (no hands or flying allowed), and it caught on fast.

As the term rolled on, and the sun sailed higher, we took to going down to the sea. After school, the whole class would take their towels to the beach below the harbour – not that it was much of a beach, just a shoreline of pebbles and shoutingly cold water. But it was fun, even though I had to teach myself to swim the hard way, swallowing a lot of water in the process.

The others could dive through the water like dolphins. They created fountains and waterspouts to make everyone shriek. Some of them liked to conjure up sea-monsters: ferocious swordfish or gigantic jellyfish, which, although they were only creatures of air and water, looked horribly real. The first time I saw one, I thrashed out of the waves in a panic, and then realised that Gowan was still in the water and helpless with laughter.

'That one got you,' he gasped.

'You made it!' I said accusingly,

'Nah. Bruno. They're his babies.' Sure enough, the giant jellyfish entwined its tentacles lovingly around Bruno before exploding in a shower of pink bubbles. The monsters didn't last long – nothing made out of the sea did. The sea didn't take well to being magicked.

Once I watched Jay trying to hold back the waves, arms upraised: he managed it for about half a minute, and then the sea was too strong for him. I felt the commanding pull of its currents against my legs, and noted the white tongues licking the lips of each wave that yawned to swallow me. I was careful.

Since we had a couple of leaky boats, I learnt to use those too. My friends could conjure up little winds to drive them wherever they wanted, but I had to study the breezes, learning to cajole them into my sails. I decided that maybe I could be a sailor when I grew up.

I was baling out the leakier of the boats one day, when there was a commotion on shore. Cassie was jumping up and down, shouting and flapping her hands. This was so unusual that I put down my baler and stared.

'Look *out*, Bru!' she cried. 'It's not one of yours!'

I looked at Bruno, floating on a fountain of spray above the waves, dozing. I couldn't see anything wrong. Even when the sharp grey fin rose out of the sea, I assumed it was an illusion – if not Bruno's, someone else's.

'Bru!' I yelled. 'Whose is the shark?'

Bruno opened his eyes lazily, swivelled his head, and yelped. In his shock, he fell straight down into the water. The grey fin sliced towards him. Bruno surfaced, arms flailing, and screamed.

I started screeching, 'Get him out! *Shark!* Get him out!' and began to paddle to where Bruno was thrashing in the water. Before I could reach him, everyone else's magic had lifted him out and flown him through the air – with the startled shark attached to his leg – before dumping him on the beach.

The shark let go and started to gasp and heave, drowning in air. But Bruno didn't move. There was blood all over his leg.

Jay knelt beside him. 'I should have spell-checked it,' he groaned. 'I just didn't bother.'

Cassie began to wrap a towel tightly around the bleeding leg. Bruno stirred and whimpered. 'Not your fault,' she said shortly. 'My fault. I foresaw it – just not soon enough.'

'Then it's not your fault either,' said Jay.

I thought it was my fault. I'd startled Bruno so that he fell in, and then I hadn't been fast enough to get him out.

'Spread those towels, let's lift him,' ordered Jay. Cassie laid out the towels and stepped back, the crowd parting from her. She stood aside as Bruno, moaning, was gently shifted onto the towels, which rose up like a floating stretcher. They began to carry him towards the town, surrounded by anxious children.

I was left on the shore with Cassie, feeling sick and useless. I said,

'What do you mean – you *foresaw* it?'

'That's what I do,' said Cassie, her voice low. She stared down at the hissing pebbles.

'You see the future?'

'Bits of it.' She sounded very tired.

'Nobody told me. Is Bruno going to be all right?'

'I don't know. I don't see everything, only glimpses. That's bad enough.'

'Bad enough for what? You just saved Bruno's life!'

'Did I? I don't know. Sometimes it's worse if I tell people.' She fell silent, gazing out to sea. I didn't understand, so I waited.

'Five years ago,' she said, 'I foresaw our next-door neighbour lying dead on his kitchen table, in his coffin. It was that hot summer when loads of people died of heatstroke. I told my father, and he told the neighbour, and the neighbour packed up and left for the hills to avoid the heat.'

57

'So?'

'So on the way there he jumped into a pool to cool off and hit his head on a rock and died. They brought him back in his coffin.'

'Oh.'

'Yes. My mother took me round to pay our respects, and there he was laid out on the kitchen table just like I'd foreseen.' She turned a stone with her foot, sending a crab scuttling. 'So now the worse I see, the more I try not to say anything. Only sometimes I can't help it, like with Bruno just now. I didn't save his life. Everyone else did.'

'*I* didn't.' I bit my lip. 'Can you tell me something?'

'No.' She shook her head vigorously.

But I couldn't help myself. 'Will I ever be able to do magic?'

'I don't know that.'

I didn't believe her. 'We'd better get back to school,' I said, curt and disappointed. Half a mile up the road she said abruptly,

'I'll tell you one thing you'll be good at.'

'Yes?'

I was too eager. I never expected her answer. 'Playing the goosehorn,' she said.

'The goosehorn? What good is a goosehorn? How's *that* going to help me?'

'I don't know.'

'Why bother to tell me, then?' I turned on my heel and marched swiftly ahead of her, back to school.

Chapter 8

Although the gashes in Bruno's leg were easily patched by magic, he had lost a lot of blood and had to stay in the city infirmary for a while. We sneaked out at lunchtimes to take him presents. Jay made him a set of indoor fireworks to let off when the nurses weren't looking, Sandor gave him a laughing joke book, and Hanni and Marta had created a pack of dream spells.

'So you won't have nightmares about sharks,' explained Hanni.

I gave him a bag of doughnuts from a street stall. My present felt very inadequate. So did I, when all the others started doing tricks to entertain Bruno, turning his quilt into a bundle of puppies, his jug into a sherbet fountain and his bedpan into chocolate. I came away feeling more useless than ever.

I brooded on Cassie's prophecy. If I could never learn magic, never be good at anything that mattered, what was the point in trying?

So I stopped trying. I messed about, spilt ink on my books, chiselled the desks, and threw my pencils around. I stole Mr Wragg's rock collection and laid it out on the flyball pitch with a big sign: 'Free the Fossils'. I was rude to Miss Ibbs because I hated the concerned voice she kept just for me. I outdid even Gowan in cheeking teachers.

Gowan didn't like it. I saw him eyeing me with hostility. He hunted me down one lunchtime in the music room, where I was keeping the goosehorn players company. I was getting to like goosehorn music, in small doses. The players lowered their instruments as Gowan swaggered in. He said belligerently,

'Think you're cock of the school now, do you?'

'What d'you mean?' I said.

'Trying to lord it over everybody!'

Jay laughed. 'That's Gowan's job, Ned, being the big bad lad. You're beating him at the only thing he's any good at!'

'What d'you mean?' snarled Gowan in his turn.

'He didn't mean anything,' said Hanni.

'Oh, yes, he did! The only thing I'm good at, eh? What about this dribbling village idiot who can't even play flyball?'

I wasn't going to take that. I jumped on Gowan. He was bigger than me, but I got a good punch in before Hanni and Marta and Jay pulled us apart.

Gowan yelled at me, hand clutched to his chin, 'Little toad! Stinking rat! Useless worm! I *challenge* you!'

'All right,' I said. 'What to?'

'Oh no,' whispered Hanni.

Marta looked horrified. 'He means a magic duel! You mustn't accept!'

'Too late,' sneered Gowan. 'He already has.'

'Ned didn't know what you meant,' said Jay. 'Gowan, that's not fair! You should withdraw.'

60

'No way,' said Gowan. 'He agreed. It's binding.'

My mind was racing. A magical duel? A *real* one? The children back home sometimes played at duels, until Miss Plumbly caught them and sent them to stand in the corner. Those duels hadn't been serious. They'd usually involved a lot of water and mud; everyone got filthy, but nobody got hurt. I had a feeling this was different.

Gowan tossed a coin onto the floor. 'Your move,' he growled. 'No? Mine, then.'

As he stretched out his hand, I looked down in alarm. The floor tiles were pulling themselves up under my feet. I stumbled, falling backwards as tiles ripped themselves up and started to rain down on me like giant hailstones – only harder and heavier. I wrapped my arms over my head, trying to protect myself, and heard Marta shout:

'Stop it, Gowan! Mr Wragg will have a fit if you break his floor!'

'Yeah, and Kelver Truso will have a fit if you break Ned's skull!' added Jay.

'You think I care?' But the shower of tiles ceased. Peering through my fingers, I saw them sliding back into their places, and started to get off my knees.

'Oh, no, you don't!' said Gowan. 'I ain't finished yet!'

He clicked his fingers, and Jay's goosehorn ascended into the air. Its horns began to sprout leathery, scaly wings; the stops sharpened into claws.

'Hey!' cried Jay. 'That's *my* goosehorn!'

Gowan just grinned. The goosehorn was swelling

until it was ten times its normal size. Its twin trumpets blew out black smoke with an angry *whoof*, like giant nostrils. Then two flames shot out, searing my face and singeing my hair.

It was a brass dragon, ugly and deformed. It flamed again, and I threw myself to the floor as its hot breath blazed across my back.

'*Ennetti Danna*,' said Jay's voice clearly. There was a hiss and a long, rasping sigh. When I raised my head the dragon was sinking to the ground, trumpets wheezing, wings and claws shrivelling, then gone.

'That's against the rules!' shouted Gowan. 'You're not allowed to interfere!'

'That's *my* goosehorn,' said Jay coldly.

'The duel's not over! He hasn't submitted!'

'I submit,' I said, standing up. 'You are the biggest, baddest bully in the school, and your magic's much stronger than mine. Will that do?'

Gowan looked taken aback.

'You have to accept,' said Marta quickly.

'I suppose,' muttered Gowan, scratching his head. After a moment he stamped away looking baffled, as if he'd missed a trick and wasn't sure where.

'Thanks,' I said, grinning at Jay. But he didn't look happy.

'Don't try and fight any more duels! You can't win without magic. You're going to get yourself into trouble, and we might not be there next time to get you out.'

Before I could reply, Cassie burst in. Her face was

pale and shocked, as if she'd awoken in the middle of a nightmare and still had it before her eyes.

'Cass! What is it?' cried Marta. 'You look like you've seen a ghost!'

'Miss Lithgoe wants to talk to you, Ned,' Cassie said faintly.

'What for?' I was filled with sudden dread. 'What's wrong? Cass – has something happened to my family? To Uncle Kelver?'

'No. Nothing like that. It's just – another child's gone missing.'

'Cassie,' said Jay, 'what have you foreseen?'

'Nothing.' She shook her head vehemently. '*Nothing.* I've seen nothing at all.' But as she ran out, her face was twisted in anguish.

I went to Miss Lithgoe's office full of apprehension. When Miss Lithgoe saw me, a sharp line drew itself between her brows.

'Now then, Ned! We've had bad reports of your behaviour. Mr Wragg has asked me to deal with them, as he has bigger matters to see to at present. Well?'

I shuffled a bit. 'Yeah, I know. It's just that—'

'You feel frustrated by your lack of magic. That's understandable. But how exactly is messing about and disrupting classes going to help? You should be learning what you can, not fretting about what you can't.' She paused, staring into space, and I put out a surreptitious finger to check if she was really there.

She was. At once her stern gaze flew back to me.

63

'Let that be the last of it,' she said sharply. 'No more nonsense, Ned. I can't be doing with it when another child has disappeared.'

'What? *Who?*'

'Della, from the year below you.'

'Was it – the Necromancers?' I asked hesitantly.

'We don't know.'

'I always thought Necromancers were only people in stories,' I said.

She sighed and rubbed a hand across her eyes. 'So did everyone else, Ned, until recently. Oh, they used to exist back in the past: two hundred years ago, they were pirates who crossed the sea in their boats to steal food and riches from us. They would snatch unwary children to keep as slaves. We thought they'd died out... but now children have started disappearing, and nobody knows why.'

'Can't the Mages find out?'

'They're working on it,' said Miss Lithgoe grimly. 'That's what's keeping your Uncle Kelver away. It's difficult work for the Council, trying to track them down... They patrol the coasts, but there are no signs of any boats. The children just disappear into nowhere. One or two have reappeared, generally with broken bones, quite unable to say what happened. One was muttering gibberish about huge flying ships...'

'Flying ships?' I said sharply. I remembered the giant shadow that had moved across the stars as I lay in the field.

Miss Lithgoe shrugged. 'He was confused. He'd had a blow on the head. We've seen nothing to back up his story.'

'But could flying ships exist? What if they were invisible?'

'Personally, I can't imagine any way of keeping such things in the air,' said Miss Lithgoe, shaking her head. 'Nor of keeping them invisible. The power required would be immense.'

'Uncle Kelver will track them down,' I said.

'Well, if he can't, no one can. But do you understand now why I don't want you being sent to me again over silly misbehaviour?'

'Yes.'

'Here's something to keep you busy.' Reaching behind her desk, she handed over a large, black, battered case. I took it doubtfully.

'A goosehorn,' she said. 'I'm told they're tame for you. Lessons with Mr Fellows three times a week, and you can do extra practice during magic classes. I want you ready to play in the concert next month.'

'*What?*'

'Buckle down to it, Ned,' she warned me, 'or I'll be saying things I'd rather not in my next report to Kelver Truso.'

'You report to him?'

'Certainly I do. I write to him weekly. So what shall I tell him in my next message, Ned?'

'Um...'

'Quite. Pull your socks up, and practise that goose-horn.'

She shooed me out, and I walked thoughtfully back to the classroom.

News of the missing girl had just broken there. Most people were convinced the Necromancers had snatched Della, although nobody knew where or when. She'd simply gone into town one day, and never come back.

'She might have just run away,' I said.

Marta snorted. 'Why? She was perfectly happy.'

'Maybe she went to the beach and met another shark.'

Marta shook her head. 'Nobody's been swimming since Bruno got hurt. I'm telling you, it must have been the Necromancers.'

'What do they look like?' I asked.

'Nobody knows,' said Hanni. 'They're cloaked in invisibility. And they're *evil*.'

'Why would they want children as slaves?'

'Doesn't your uncle know all about them?'

'He hasn't told me,' I said. I decided that Uncle Kelver must have been trying to protect me from worry.

But Marta said impatiently, 'I expect that's because you haven't got any magic. It's all to do with magic, so you wouldn't understand about it. What are you doing with that goosehorn case, Ned?'

'It's mine,' I said. I knelt to open the case. Although its outside was scarred, inside was unfaded blue velvet as bright as the summer sky. The goosehorn nestled there snugly until Marta touched it, when it arched and squirmed. I laid my hand upon it, and it was still again.

'It *likes* you,' said Marta, indignant. 'That is so unfair! I was dying to learn, and they made me give up after one lesson.'

'It doesn't *like* me,' I said. 'It just doesn't know I'm there. Because I've got no magic.' I closed the case with a thud. I didn't want to play the goosehorn. I wanted to be with Uncle Kelver, tracking down Necromancers, helping him through difficulty and danger.

'Are you going to learn to play it?' Marta asked in disbelief.

'I'll have to,' I said reluctantly. 'It's all I've got.'

Chapter 9

Days passed with no news of Della, but no more
vanishings either. Gradually people forgot to be scared.
As for me, I was too busy to worry about mythical
kidnappers.

I was determined that Miss Lithgoe's next report to
Uncle Kelver would be a good one. Although I
desperately wished I could help Uncle Kelver,
wherever he was, I knew that without magic I wouldn't
be much use to him. All I could do was to try not to
disappoint him.

So I knuckled down to my schoolwork again. I had a
load to catch up on, and goosehorn practice to endure. If
the goosehorn was the only thing I could ever be good
at, then I'd make sure I was the best. Unfortunately, no
matter how much I practised, it still brayed like a
disgruntled donkey. The only consolation was that
everyone else's sounded even worse, while they had a
much harder struggle to play it.

'I've never met anything so *strong*,' panted Jay,
sitting on the horse trough, trying to stop his goosehorn
turning itself inside out. 'The concert's only a week
away, and this stupid thing won't let me practise! How
do you do it?'

'I think it lets me play it because I don't use magic.
Could you try not using magic?'

'I can't not use magic! You might as well say don't breathe, or don't hear!'

'Well, just use as little as possible,' I suggested. 'Don't try so hard. Think of something else.'

'What?'

'I don't know. Food, or something.'

'Huh!' Jay laid the writhing horn on the cobbles. As it stilled, he looked away, humming. Then, still humming, he picked it up casually. The goosehorn twitched, but didn't try to throttle him when he hoisted it onto his shoulder, carelessly whistling. Jay turned the whistle into a puff at the mouthpiece, as if by accident. The goosehorn honked melodiously. Jay turned to me, beaming.

'It worked!' he said. 'I thought of all the different doughnut fillings I could, and it worked!' The goosehorn uncurled its left trumpet and whacked him in the ribs. Jay swore.

'Don't give up!' I said. 'You nearly had it.'

'Stupid beast,' grumbled Jay, but he tried again and this time managed a dozen notes before the horn rebelled. He couldn't refrain from using magic for longer. 'It's like holding your breath,' he said. 'You have to give in.'

But at least Jay and his goosehorn both stayed in one piece until the concert. He passed the word on, and soon I found myself tutoring Hanni and Rollo and others in not using magic with their goosehorns.

This concert, I gathered, was a big occasion. There was a festival in the Plaza – some ancient tradition – and the goosehorn band was supposed to be the highlight.

69

Why, I couldn't imagine. I hoped the audience would bring earplugs.

Jay offered me a lift to the Plaza on a carpet, but I turned it down. The school carpets were threadbare and spellbound, not a good combination for someone who couldn't fly. So that summer's afternoon I set off walking with my horn under my arm while a procession of rugs, rafts and armchairs flew past overhead. There was even one girl on a broomstick, looking dreadfully uncomfortable.

The Plaza was buzzing. I hadn't expected this huge crowd of townspeople, seemingly thousands of them, milling about with pies and candyfloss. As a swarm of music stands glided in and were directed to their places by a harassed Mr Wragg, my stomach curled itself into a nervous ball and tried to hide in my throat.

Eventually, the whole band was settled beneath the giant statue of Leode, which stared indifferently over our heads. We began to play.

As soon as our twenty-four goosehorns started up, the crowd stopped milling and eating, and paid attention. Boy, did they pay attention. They couldn't do anything else. Although my stomach was still curled in a frightened ball, my fingers managed to hit most of the right notes. Out of the corner of my eye I saw Jay fighting with his horn; he'd obviously failed to think of enough doughnut fillings. One girl got completely overpowered and had to be prised from her goosehorn's grip and carried away.

By the interval everyone was exhausted and sweating, including the stunned audience. Jay looked totally hacked off. He dropped his coiling goosehorn on his chair, rasped, 'I'm going for a drink,' and disappeared in the direction of the fountain. Ten minutes later, when Mr Wragg ordered everyone back to their seats for the second bout of horn-wrestling, Jay hadn't come back. I wasn't too surprised.

Cassie pushed through the audience. 'Jay's gone!' she hissed.

'Yeah, he got fed up. He scarpered.'

'No! He's been *taken*!'

'What?'

The band started up again with a raucous fanfare that blotted out her reply. She mouthed at me. 'Necromancers!'

'*What?*'

She pulled me off my chair into the crowd and bellowed in my ear. 'He disappeared from the fountain! One minute there, the next not! He just *went*!'

'Playing tricks,' I yelled back.

'*No!* They've *taken* him!'

'So where are these Necromancers?' I demanded. 'Have you seen them?'

Cassie nodded; shook her head, nodded again. At a pause in the honking while everyone turned their pages, she whispered, 'I've *foreseen* them. They've taken Jay.'

'No,' I said. The day was too ordinary, the crowd too big, Jay too grouchy for me to believe any of this. Thrusting my horn under my arm, I began to push through the crowd, away from the goosehorn disaster area. 'I'll look for him. I bet he's hanging around somewhere, laughing at us.'

'*No!* Ned, you must go back to school – otherwise they'll take you too!'

I was annoyed. I didn't want to be frightened like this. 'Why should they?'

'I've foreseen it!'

'If you foresaw all this, why didn't you tell us?'

'I only saw bits. I thought if I said nothing, nothing might happen . . .'

'So what happens to me?'

'I don't know,' said Cassie.

By this time I had reached the fountain. There was no sign of Jay. 'Come on, you must have some idea what happens next. You've foreseen it!'

'I've seen nothing,' said Cassie, and she began to shake. 'Nothing happens.' I began to answer, but the manic blaring of the goosehorns killed my words. Cassie put her mouth close to my ear, so that her voice spoke inside my head.

'My foresight stops here. I can see nothing beyond this day. There is nothing else – just blackness. There's no future. It's the end of everything, Ned. It's *death*.'

I looked back at the candyflossed crowd. Everything was bright and normal, if ear-splittingly loud. What did she mean? Whose death? I didn't want to believe any of it.

But when I turned to challenge Cassie, she was gone.

And then I was gone. And the world was gone. There was nothing but blackness. It was the end of everything.

72

Chapter 10

I was wrong. There *was* something. Air was rushing past me, though I was blind and stifled as if a blanket wrapped me tight.

With a huge effort I opened my eyes, and saw the Plaza falling away beneath me with sickening swiftness. The goosehorns' honking faded rapidly: the crowd didn't look up as I was hauled into the sky.

They couldn't see me. The iridescent shimmer around me told me I was inside a shield of invisibility. If anyone had seen me vanish, they would just have thought – look, another player skiving off, don't blame the poor kid.

I rolled my eyes upwards. Above me hung something massive and almost invisible, only the sun looked thin and unconvincing through it, and the clouds didn't quite fit.

It was getting closer. The air stopped rushing and I thudded to my knees on an unseen surface. I was gasping just like when I first went in the sea and thought I was drowning.

Somebody pushed me in the back, so that I tumbled forward, scraping past a doorway, and sprawled on the ground. At once my surroundings became visible.

A wooden floor, not very clean. Lamplight, weak. Several pairs of leather boots, scuffed, all pointing at me.

I was grabbed by my hair and dragged to my feet.

Bearded faces scowled down at me. There were half a dozen men, wearing chain mail over dirty leather jerkins, long knives stuck in their belts. One of them held Cassie, twisting her arm behind her back.

'Two more for the galley,' he sneered. 'Come to join our happy band, have you?'

I was in a long room, lit only by a few small, round windows; their tiny, dazzling discs of sunlight hardly penetrated the darkness below. Then, as my eyes adjusted, I saw rows of children huddled miserably on benches, staring at their laps.

'Get over there!' my captor said, thrusting me onto a bench. The children shuffled along to make room without looking up. Cassie was bundled onto another bench nearby.

My mind was racing. A galley? That meant a ship, with rows of men heaving at the oars. But in this long, dark room, there were no men apart from scruffy guards. There were only children, and no one held an oar.

Instead, the boy next to me held a toy boat. It was a rough plaster model, with three sticks for masts; but he cradled it as if it was made of spun glass, fragile and precious. I realised that all the children in my row crouched over identical boats. A guard shoved one into my hands.

'You fly that,' he commanded.

I almost laughed aloud. What *was* this? Glancing around, I spotted Jay behind me, staring at his boat with a terrified gaze. Maybe the boats were bewitched. Or maybe the children were – for none of them spoke, or looked at anything except the model boats on their knees. They must contain some magic power that I couldn't detect.

So I sat with my boat in my lap like the others until the guards moved away. Then I whispered to my neighbour, 'What's this for?' and jiggled it.

'Careful!' he hissed. 'If you break it they'll throw you off the ship!'

'So this *is* a ship?'

'Ssh! Airship,' he muttered. 'It sails by magic – *our* magic. We have to keep it afloat, by doing flying spells on these boats. The magic keeps the airship in the sky.' His lips moved silently, chanting spells.

I looked around at the other children doing the same. They looked as exhausted as if they really were pulling on heavy oars: galley slaves driving the ship with the power not of their muscles, but of their magic.

Only, of course, I had no magic. The little boat sat on my knee like an unwanted birthday present. Bowing my head, I pretended to murmur spells like all the rest, and hoped the guards wouldn't notice. After all, how could they tell the difference? They slouched against the wall, chatting and laughing, and occasionally flicking their whips at the unfortunate children closest to them.

I caught Jay's eye. He tried to smile, but couldn't. I had never seen Jay look scared before – I didn't think he could get scared. I twisted round to count the children: about sixty, I decided, and then realised with a shock that more were lying down at the back, apparently sleeping.

The guard cuffed my head back round. I sat still, muttering fake spells and wondering what to do. Time passed: I couldn't guess how long. Long enough to get thirsty, and for my back to ache and my legs to stiffen.

'All change, brats!' yelled a guard with a fierce moustache and one golden earring. He kicked at the limp bodies on the floor until they struggled to their feet, coughing. Listlessly they swapped places with the first two rows of children, who trooped to the back and immediately slumped to the floor, worn out.

The changeover was too slow. I felt the ship begin a slow fall, and through the portholes saw the clouds drift upwards.

'*Move* it!' yelled the angry guards, whipping the new team into place. One small girl, hollow-eyed with exhaustion, lolled on her bench, eyes closed. Between her thin hands, her model boat was crumbling. The stern had broken away; two of the masts had fallen out.

'Oi!' A fat guard snatched it up. 'You're not trying, are you? What's this rubbish?' As the boat fell apart, he flung it down with an oath.

'I'll chuck her out,' said Golden Earring. Dragging the girl to her feet, he manhandled her through the door.

I looked at my neighbour. 'What'll he do?'

'Throw her overboard.'

'What!' Then I remembered that of course the little girl could fly. No problem. She'd just glide down to earth, safe and free.

Or would she? *Could* she fly, exhausted as she was?

Since I couldn't fly myself, I had no idea. I glanced over at Cassie, wanting an answer, but her eyes were fixed on the door, her lips moving. A corner of her boat, unheeded in her lap, flaked away as she chanted.

I guessed what she was doing. She was using her magic to keep the girl afloat. And because her spells weren't working on her model ship, it was starting to disintegrate. That was the warning sign that the slaves weren't doing their job properly.

I looked down at my own boat with new alarm, and to my horror, saw that the masts were already loose. A crumb of plaster fell from the boat's side. I tried to stick it back with a damp finger, and it promptly fell off again, followed by another, bigger flake.

What had Cassie said? There was no future. Did she mean no future for *me*? I felt hot and shaky. What would happen if I got discovered and thrown overboard? I couldn't fly down! My boat was my livelihood, my future, and it was breaking up before my eyes.

I nursed my little boat as if I loved it, shielding it from the guards while I chanted. When lumps of tough bread and dried fish were handed round, I folded the boat into my shirt to hide it as I ate: when, a weary while later, I was ordered with the rest of my row to lie down and sleep, I hugged it gently to my chest like a favourite, worn-out toy.

I did not sleep. The blood-red glow of sunset filled the hold, so that it seemed like the belly of some huge sea-beast, full of poor swallowed sailors who could only

77

sigh out their misery. I lay still, listening to the sad, heavy breath of my companions, holding my fragile boat together with my fingers, feeling it slowly turn to powder in my hands.

Chapter 11

I had barely begun to doze when an oath and a sharp kick jolted me fully awake. 'Get up, you useless scum!'

As I staggered to my feet, my boat – a boat no longer – slid to the ground in a little heap of dust and grit.

'What's *that* meant to be?' the fat guard roared. 'Haven't been trying, have you, brat! Ready to go overboard, are you?'

'No! I *was* trying! I just can't do magic.'

'Liar! Everyone can do magic. You're going over.'

'But it's true!'

'It's true,' said Jay behind me. The guard turned round and hit him.

'Shut it, or you'll go over too!'

But Golden Earring eyed me thoughtfully. 'Wait ... I reckon this one should go to Lady Galera. She might be interested. She'll sort him out, anyway.'

The fat guard laughed, nastily. 'That's for sure! Let's have you, scum!'

He bundled me outside, onto a narrow platform overhung by the swollen arc of the ship's body. A rusty ladder crawled up the ship's side, and the guard prodded me to climb it. The cold wind tugged at me. The last sliver of sun was gliding down behind the distant hills. As I climbed, I tried not to look down at the tiny fields stitched together far below.

Reaching the top, I scrambled over a rail onto the deck. This was the biggest ship I had ever seen – complete with lifeboats, anchors, ropes piled in neat coils, and a full set of sails stiffening in the sharp breeze. A handful of sailors paused in reefing the sails to stare, as the guard, puffing after his climb, marched me over the bleached deck.

'Move it!' He shoved me down a gangway, and into a stateroom, panelled and polished so that candlelight shone back from every surface. By the table stood a man and a woman, consulting maps.

The guard cleared his throat nervously. 'Excuse me, my lady? It's that last slave we picked up. He *says* he's got no magic. Thought you might like to see him before we throw him overboard.'

Lady Galera turned, frowning. She was lean and elegant, with the wide eyes and cold stare of a cat.

'No magic?' Her voice was as sharp and cold as a knife blade.

'That's what he *says*.'

'All right. Leave him here. You can go.' She stalked around me coolly, a cat inspecting a captive mouse. Then, without warning, she flung her hand out at my face. I winced back, as a jolt like electricity made my skin tingle and my hair stand on end.

Lady Galera hadn't touched me. She withdrew her hand, clenched in a fist, slowly opened it, and looked, and laughed.

'Would you believe it, Rendel? Not a spark.'

'No magic at all?' said her companion disbelievingly.

'The boy's a freak!' It had taken her five seconds to discover what had taken the Mages a good fifteen minutes. She stalked around me again, eyes narrowed.

'You were taken from Leodwych Plaza,' she said, 'weren't you? With *that*.' She pointed, and I saw my goosehorn propped behind the door. 'Which means the school: which means magic.'

'So he *must* have magic,' said Rendel.

'What's your name, boy? Tell.' She raised one finger, and my mouth opened against my will. I couldn't stop the words from leaking out.

'Ned Truso.'

Her eyes narrowed. 'Truso? As in the Mage, Kelver Truso?'

'He's my cousin.' I would rather have denied it, but I found I had no choice. I hoped it wouldn't cause trouble for Uncle Kelver.

'Well, well! Cousin to the famous Mage.' A thin smile crept across her lips. 'I don't think we'll dispose of you just yet, Ned Truso.'

'My lady!' objected Rendel. 'The ship is already labouring, without any dead weight crew. Pickings have been poor this trip. We've not taken enough slaves to keep us going. The boy should be thrown out, or sent back to the galley. Are you *sure* he's got no magic? I've never heard of such a thing!'

'But I have, Rendel,' said Lady Galera. 'Just fancy! A Mage's cousin with no magic.' She became brisk. 'We're heading seawards now. In a few hours we can

81

safely shed our invisibility shield and jettison our wastes. That'll relieve the drain on our power.'

'But it'll mean no new slaves until we're back over land,' grumbled Rendel. 'We're wearing them out faster than we can replace them. We can't let this boy sit around doing nothing!'

'Hadrel can have him. Yes. I'll give him to Hadrel. Summon him now, will you?'

Rendel did not look pleased. But he picked up a little bell from the table and shook it once, soundlessly. A moment later a boy appeared in the doorway. He looked younger than me, I thought, but taller and thinner, lank-haired, and sulky as a camel.

'I wish you wouldn't summon me that way,' he complained in a high-pitched voice. 'Why can't you send a servant?'

'I'll transubstantiate you next time if you don't like it,' said Lady Galera sharply. Then she softened her voice. 'Something for you, Hadrel. You're always saying you want your own servant. Well, here you are! You can have *this* one.'

Hadrel glared down his nose at me. 'He looks like one of the galley slaves.'

'He is. But this one can't do magic.'

Hadrel drew back indignantly. 'Why would I want a failed galley slave? Especially one with no magic.'

'Because,' said Lady Galera with slow impatience, 'a servant with no power can do you no harm, can he, Hadrel?'

'*No one* can do me any harm,' retorted Hadrel.

'Are you quite sure of that? Take him away. You may experiment on him, but don't kill him. And don't maim him too badly; we might want him later.'

'What for?'

'Take that instrument of his too. Look after it! It's a goosehorn – I believe they're totally impossible to play, but rather valuable.'

'A goosehorn!' Hadrel's suspicious eyes widened. He snatched it up greedily, whereupon it came to life and tried to tie itself around his neck.

Hadrel tapped it lightly with one finger, and it stiffened, frozen into an unnatural coil. I'd never seen anyone do that to a goosehorn before – not even Miss Lithgoe.

'What's your name, slave?' he demanded.

'Ned.' This time, I couldn't have added Truso if I'd wanted. Lady Galera smiled.

'Come on, then, Donkey Ned,' said Hadrel. 'Follow me.'

I followed him out and down a narrow passage, watching the back of his head. 'Excuse me?'

'What is it, Donkey?'

'You're being a bit careless. I could biff you on the head now and you'd never know a thing,' I said. 'Just a friendly warning from a loyal slave.'

'Just try it,' said Hadrel without turning round. 'Go on.' I hesitated.

'Go *on*,' he repeated. So I aimed a punch at his head.

My hand bounced away before it even touched his hair.

'All right,' I said, rubbing my hand, 'you're shielded, but what if I could break the shield?'

'You'd need stronger magic than mine,' retorted Hadrel, 'and nobody on board has *that* except Galera.'

'Is Lady Galera your mother?'

'She is *not*.' Fiercely kicking open a cabin door, he clomped inside.

I hardly knew where to put my feet. Hadrel's cabin was very small, very untidy, and had a very odd smell. Clothes were flung across the floor, books and candle ends were strewn upon the bed, there were dirty cups rolling on the table and dirty sacks lolling underneath it; and against one wall were stacked small cages, four high.

I peered inside a cage and wished I hadn't. A sad-eyed animal – its front half mouse, its rear half frog – blinked back at me. The other cages held rat-lizards, winged rabbits, a poor ferret dragging a snake's tail...I moved away quickly.

Hadrel swept some books off the bed and sat down.

'Show me how to play this goosehorn,' he commanded.

'It's the wrong shape right now.' As I took the goosehorn, it unfroze and relaxed back into its normal shape, lifeless as always for me. I slung it over my shoulder, fingered the stops and launched into 'Leode's March'. The cups on the table rattled. Hadrel listened intently, without even wincing. Then he signalled me to stop.

'Right, I've got that. Give it here.' He froze it again

84

before it could squirm out of shape, settled it into position, and blew.

It yowled like a dog with its head in a bucket. The half-mice cowered in their cages. He tried again, and a rat-toad keeled over in a dead faint.

'Ow,' I said, involuntarily.

Hadrel glowered. 'Well, how come *you* can play it, Donkey? You haven't even got magic!'

'You don't need magic to play it.'

'You must! Goosehorns are famous for being magical! Leode invented them, didn't he? Galera says I've got nearly as much magic as Leode had. I think I might even have more.'

'Who is Lady Galera, if she isn't your mother?' I asked cautiously.

'She's the captain, because she's got the most magic. *I'll* be captain when I'm older and more powerful than her.'

'So the most powerful person gets to be captain?'

'Well, of *course*!' said Hadrel with contempt. 'The stronger your magic, the bigger the ship you command. And this is the biggest.'

'That's a weird system.'

'Everyone uses that system. It's the only one that works. Got no magic, you're nowhere,' said Hadrel. 'In *our* country people without much magic have to farm the fields, stay where they belong. In the mud.'

I considered the school, ruled by Mr Wragg, desperate to be a Mage, hopeless at teaching; and Leodwych, ruled

85

by the Council of Mages – including Uncle Kelver, who was powerful enough for even Lady Galera to have heard of him. Maybe everyone did use that system. It didn't leave much room for *me*.

So I had better make myself useful. 'Shall I tidy those books up?' I offered. My mother would have been amazed.

'I suppose you might as well.'

I began to pick up books. They weren't spell-books, but stories. 'How long have you been on the ship?' I asked, since Hadrel seemed willing to talk. You might almost have thought he was lonely.

'I was chosen four years ago.'

'What for? Who chose you?'

'I was chosen as next captain because of my magic potential,' he said proudly. 'Syron found me. He's the most powerful wizard I know, even more powerful than Galera. He says I'll be more powerful than Galera too. But I reckon I'll be even better than him, one day.' He wasn't boasting. He believed it.

'So you've been on the boat for four years?'

'We don't sail all the time, only in summer. In winter we go back home.'

'Where's home?'

'East, across the sea.'

'The maps at school don't show anything there!'

'Well, of course not,' said Hadrel smugly. 'As far as *you're* concerned, there is nothing there. We make sure that any boats coming our way get stuck in fog banks. If

86

they get through those, we do a little illusion to make them think our country's nothing but swamp.'

'That's a *little* illusion?'

'We are a powerful people.' He smiled.

'Apart from your farmers.'

'Farming's for stupid people. Why get your hands dirty when you don't need to? With our airships we can get everything we need – food, drink, money, slaves. We can pick just them up as we sail along, and there's not a single thing those stupid landlubbers down below can do about it.'

'You steal them, you mean,' I said.

'Of course we do! Better than breaking your back in the fields all day. Syron rescued me from all that.'

'So are your family farmers?'

His smile vanished. 'Stop asking so many questions! Go away now. I want to sleep.'

'Where shall I sleep?'

'Not in here! In the bathroom, I suppose,' he said sulkily.

The bathroom, through a small door, contained a discreet bucket and a copper bathtub. At a click of Hadrel's fingers the towels leapt off the floor and flew into the air over the tub, to form a swinging white hammock that was tied to nothing. I climbed up into it gingerly. It swayed but didn't fall.

'Won't it dump me in the bath?'

'Eight-hour spell,' said Hadrel shortly, and disappeared into his cabin.

I lay in my towelling hammock, which smelt of alien soap, and listened to the faint noises which signified his going to bed. After a while I rolled carefully out of the hammock and began to creep towards the door.

I didn't even get halfway before I bounced off an invisible surface, hard as rubber, slippery as ice. It surrounded the hammock on all sides like a giant bubble. I supposed that was part of the eight-hour spell too.

I climbed back into the hammock and rocked in the lamplight, wondering why Hadrel hadn't made me sleep on the floor like the galley slaves. Had he made the hammock out of kindness – or just to show off? I remembered the half-mice, and shivered. What sort of person would want to make *those*?

Then my thoughts stepped back to Jay and Cassie, curled on the galley floor, protecting their little boats, weary and afraid. I had to help them. If only Uncle Kelver could track me down again, I thought, swoop on the boat to rescue us all with a single laughing word...

But Kelver was miles away. It was up to me – yet what could I do? I was a prisoner, although my prison was much snugger than the galley; so snug that my eyes kept closing against my will. I felt ashamed of being so warm and comfortable even as I drifted off to sleep.

Chapter 12

Next thing I knew, there was a clang and I was sitting in the bathtub. Hadrel stood in the doorway, rubbing his eyes crossly.

'*Out,*' he said. 'I want to wash. You can tidy my room.'

I retreated to his cabin. Dawn beamed through the porthole. I stacked plates and picked up clothes to fold them neatly.

Then, prompted by the smell, I cleaned out the cages of the friendlier looking creatures. Luckily they had all survived the goosehorn. Although I discovered oats and nuts in the sacks beneath the table, I wasn't sure which animals to feed them to. What did a half-frog half-mouse eat? How did it *know* what to eat? What sort of animals did these think they were?

Feeling indignant on their behalf, I plucked one out of its cage and stroked it gently. Too clammy for a mouse, too furry for a frog.

I realised that Hadrel stood behind me. 'Put it back,' he said coldly.

I obeyed. 'Why did you make them?'

'Shut up.' He clicked his fingers, and half a loaf and a slab of ham appeared on the bed. I realised I was starving. 'My breakfast,' said Hadrel. He clicked again, and a couple of ship's biscuits clattered to the floor. '*Your* breakfast. Direct from the stores. I don't like eating breakfast with the officers; they're not respectful enough.'

'Thanks.' Respectfully, I gnawed at the rock-hard biscuit, and eyed Hadrel's ham, wondering if it had been stolen from my farm. Then I thought of Jay and Cassie, nibbling on dried fish and stale bread.

I had to help them. That meant either getting away from Hadrel – which might be difficult – or somehow persuading Hadrel to help them too.

'Do you ever go down to the galley?' I asked.

'What for?'

'Have you seen the children down there? The slaves?'

He shrugged. 'Their own stupid fault for getting caught.'

'Trapped,' I said. 'Kidnapped.'

'I wouldn't let it happen to *me*. Anyway, they're not there for ever.'

'You know what happens to them if they stop working?'

'Get their memories altered, and get to go home, lucky bleeders,' said Hadrel, frowning.

'If they've got the strength to fly there safely.'

'Well, tough.'

'Do you know what it's like down in the galley?'

Hadrel threw his bread across the room. 'Do you think I care?' he exploded. 'Aren't I stuck in the same boat? Aren't I working hard enough myself, steering the ship and keeping the shield up? You think it's *easy*, making a ship this size invisible?'

'You're doing that?'

'Of course I'm doing that! Well, so is Galera – but I do most of it, so don't tell *me* about galley slaves!' Hadrel stomped over to retrieve his bread. Before he could eat it, a brass bell materialised beside his left ear and rang piercingly.

Hadrel swore. 'Damn. Galera wants me. I hate that bell!'

He slouched off down the corridor. I found myself being pulled after him as if on an invisible string. Emerging on deck, I winced; the sky was too clean and bright, the sun too close. The wind bounced off me playfully and whistled in the rigging.

When I glanced over the rail, the view took my breath away. There was no sign of Leodwych or any other town: just shrunken, huddled villages, and lanes wriggling like worms round miniature fields. And to the east stretched the sea, attached to the land by a lacy fringe of tiny, crawling waves.

Lady Galera, standing pirate-like at the prow, lowered her telescope.

'Are you pleased with your new servant, Hadrel?' she enquired.

'He talks too much.'

'Well, don't get rid of him yet. Syron might like to see him.' Hadrel grunted, and Lady Galera compressed her lips impatiently. 'Do you have to grunt and slouch like that?'

'I can stand how I like.'

'Do try to act the part, Hadrel, unless you want the crew to think you're a complete slob.'

'Did you order me up just to tell me that?'

'Of course not. As you would have noticed if you bothered to check, we're heading east. You can drop the shield when we're well out to sea.'

'Whereabouts are we?'

Lady Galera sighed in exasperation. 'For heaven's sake, Hadrel, is that the question of a future captain? Your captaincy is a *very* long way away, I can tell you that! How can you navigate if you don't study the maps?'

'Is that all?' said Hadrel. 'Can I go now?'

'In a minute.' She closed up her telescope. 'How are you getting on with the goosehorn, Hadrel?'

'Fine.' Hadrel's face was stony.

'I believe they're incredibly difficult instruments to control.'

'Not at all.'

'And impossible to play.'

'No problem.'

'Good! You must play for Syron when he comes.' Lady Galera's scornful smile told me that she must have heard Hadrel's efforts on my goosehorn. If her cabin was anywhere near his, she could hardly have avoided it. Hadrel turned abruptly on his heel and marched away.

'That's it,' he muttered. 'I'll learn to play that stinking goosehorn if it kills me. And I'll practise where *she* can't hear me.' He stamped back to his cabin, tripping over his own legs and banging his head on the lintel. I scurried after him, helpless as a puppy on an invisible lead.

Retrieving the goosehorn from under his bed amidst a

cloud of fluff, Hadrel carried it to the ship's stern deck. There he flung open a hatch and ordered me down a ladder that led into darkness. I found myself in a large hold, nearly empty but for a few limp sacks.

'Syron's bringing more supplies soon,' said Hadrel. 'We didn't get enough at Leodwych.'

Didn't *steal* enough, I nearly said, before my attention was caught by a row of tools hanging from nails on the wall. Harpoons, a trident, ropes, a saw, an axe . . . Surely I could use those for something?

I was trying to work out what, when Hadrel growled, 'Don't even think it. Those aren't going anywhere.'

He lit the lamps and let the hatch thud shut. 'No one will disturb us in here. I don't want an audience for this goosehorn. But down here' – he hoisted the axe from its nail – 'down *here,* no one can hear it scream.'

Waving the axe over the goosehorn, he bawled at it. 'You want to keep both horns? You play for me or you'll be a one-horn wonder!'

He dropped the axe to seize the goosehorn, which squirmed and fought back more fiercely than ever. It didn't like being bullied by Hadrel any more than it had by Bruno. Eventually Hadrel managed to freeze it into position. He took a deep breath, and blew.

I don't know how to describe it. Imagine a giant pig with a really bad stomach problem squealing in a cellar. Not even Jay had ever managed to get a noise like that out of a goosehorn. And the harder Hadrel tried, the worse it got.

'You want the axe?' he yelled at it.

'Hadrel, that won't work.'

Hadrel turned on me. 'Tell me what will, then!' he roared.

'I could teach you – for a price.'

'What price?'

'Two of my friends are galley slaves. You could set them free.'

'No way!'

'Then no deal,' I said.

'Good,' said Hadrel sullenly. 'I'll work this goose-horn out for myself.'

'No, you won't.'

'I will! My magic can do anything!'

'Except play the goosehorn.'

'*Anything!* I can do anything at all, more than you can anyway, you stupid, stinking turnip-head!'

That annoyed me. 'I'm not, and you can't!'

Hadrel's face was red with fury. 'Are you *challenging* me?'

'You mean to a duel?'

'Of course I mean to a duel, you donkey!' His voice was quivering with anger. It was the goosehorn he really wanted to fight, or maybe Lady Galera. I just happened to be handy. But I stood up and faced him squarely.

'All right,' I said. 'I challenge you. If I win, you have to set my friends free. If I lose, you get to keep the goosehorn and I'll teach you to play it.'

'I'm keeping it anyway, turnip-head. But you won't win.'

'Do you *agree*?'

'Yes, yes! I agree!'

'Right. Toss a coin to see who starts,' I said. I knew it was hopeless: I couldn't fight a magic duel without magic. I hadn't a chance.

But neither had Cassie or Jay, and I didn't know what else I could do.

Chapter 13

Hadrel didn't bother tossing a coin. As soon as I saw him pull a rope and a trident from the wall, I realised that he wasn't going to follow any rules. I wondered how badly he would be prepared to hurt me.

He hurled the rope at me, and I leapt back. As it hit the ground, it turned into a snake, slithering rapidly towards my feet. Surprised that he hadn't thought of something more original, I jumped over it and snatched the axe from the floor. Once you've had snakes growing out of your head, a single one on the ground isn't too scary. I swung the axe and cut it in half.

Immediately, each half began to grow a new head or tail. So I chopped those off before they properly formed, and cut off the next set of heads that sprouted too; and wondered when Hadrel was going to think of something different, because I was quite happy to keep chopping off snakes' heads for as long as he wanted to make them.

He thought of something different. The axe pulsed in my hand. Its iron blade thickened, growing bristles and ears. As I hastily flung it away, the handle was already swelling into a muscled body with budding legs. It landed heavily and stood up, snorting: a wild boar, bad-temperedly shaking its head. Its tusks and feet were still forming, but in a moment it would charge.

Well, that wasn't so bad. I'd met boars in the woods

at home, and knew how to handle them. I ran to seize a harpoon, thankful that at least there wasn't room for Hadrel to create a dragon down here. I hoped he didn't think of a tiger. I didn't fancy a tiger.

As the boar charged, I dropped to my knees, bracing the harpoon. A real boar would have wheeled round and gone at me from the side. This one, not so clever, ran straight onto the harpoon, letting out a terrible squeal like a deflating balloon – and was slowly lifted up into the air.

Not by me. I had to release the harpoon, because it was transforming: becoming longer and thicker, sprouting branches and leaves. While Hadrel chanted, arms outstretched, the harpoon grew long roots that caught and strangled the headless snakes still writhing on the floor, and tried to catch and strangle my feet too. Grinning, I danced over the roots to get the saw. I could deal with a *tree*.

I was too cocky. The harpoon-tree whipped its prickly arms around me, choking the breath out of me, while I kicked and struggled. A branch tightened about my throat until white flashes appeared before my eyes.

Tearing at the clutching branches, I hoarsely shouted a spell I'd often heard Jay use. It was a firework spell. I don't even know why I said it. I suppose I thought in my desperation that Jay's magic might work on it somehow. It didn't, of course. Even as I rasped the words I knew nothing would happen.

Nothing did – except that Hadrel was startled into

jerking his head round briefly, just in case something appeared behind him. For that instant, the harpoon-tree released its grip, and I was able to wrench free.

But Hadrel had realised his mistake. As I reached for the saw, it was already starting to change. Its teeth grew longer and yellower, set in a scaly, brown jaw while it extended into a long, scaly body to match. The crocodile snapped noisily, trying out its new teeth. It began to waddle towards me, and I backed away towards the ladder.

Hadrel hurled the trident to cut off my escape. Whistling through the air at first, it braked as it began to sprout broad wings of coarse green feathers. Its three prongs swelled into heads with greedy, beady eyes and short, hooked beaks. I wondered what sort of bird it was meant to be. The heads didn't look right somehow.

'Budgie?' I said doubtfully.

'Eagle, you idiot!' yelled Hadrel. In a flurry of feathers, the wings lengthened, and the beaks grew fiercer. The scrawny necks extended until the three-headed bird was more vulture than anything else.

It swooped clumsily at my head, missed when I ducked, and landed on the crocodile. The crocodile whipped its head round fast and snapped, getting a mouthful of feathers. Two of the vulture heads pecked it vengefully while the third screeched. Hadrel was shouting – curses or charms, I couldn't tell, but it didn't help.

'Nice vulture,' I said.

'It's an *eagle*!' he bawled. 'And you're a *donkey*!'

The air shimmered as if it had been oiled. When it cleared again, everything looked different.

The room seemed much wider. I could see almost round to the back of my head, but all the colours had gone. I looked down and saw grey hooves and shaggy legs. I remember just an instant of surprise. After that it didn't seem at all strange. I was a donkey, and a donkey was what I was.

Although I could no longer think in words, I was aware that the two creatures fighting each other were not friendly and that the human opposite was an enemy. Worse – he had a whip.

I don't know where Hadrel got the whip from; I expect he transformed a headless snake. As a donkey, I didn't care, I just knew that I didn't like it. My ears went back, and my back legs twitched. There was a lot of power in those legs, just waiting to be used, so I used it.

I jumped over to Hadrel and kicked him into the corner. He made a sort of 'Whoof' noise as my hooves connected with his stomach. Then I kicked the crocodile in the teeth, and bit the middle neck of the vulture – pleased to find how long and strong my own teeth were – and then, after kicking the crocodile a couple more times, I galloped over to where Hadrel lay in the corner, ready to trample on him a bit. Next thing I knew I was a boy again.

I was quite sorry. I'd been enjoying being a donkey. Annoyed, I growled at Hadrel, 'You're down, and I win.'

I didn't expect him to agree. I expected him to leap up and fight. But Hadrel stayed down, groaning and clutching his stomach, while the crocodile and vulture began to shrivel back to their original sizes.

'You've broken all my ribs!' moaned Hadrel.

'That's what donkeys do,' I said. 'Give in?'

'I give in,' said Hadrel sulkily. 'Help me up. I can't *move*.'

I gave him a hand. 'You'll be all right. You can use magic to mend your ribs. What about my friends?'

'I can't free them.'

'You promised!'

'The guards won't let me. They'll tell Galera.'

'Oh, right,' I said. 'Of course, you wouldn't want to do anything to upset Lady Galera.'

'Wouldn't I just,' said Hadrel, his eyes flashing.

'Then use your magic to get round the guards! Surely you can think of a way! I thought you were a real magical hotshot? Or don't you mean to keep your word?'

He put his shoulders back, wincing proudly. 'I'll keep my word. I'm a man of honour. What are your friends called?'

'Jay and Cassie.'

'If I summon them, you won't mention the duel?'

'Not a word.'

'And you must leave the ship straight away. I can tell Galera you jumped overboard. She'll be furious,' he said with satisfaction.

I agreed. I felt bad about the other galley slaves – but

there was a limit to what I could ask. l wasn't convinced Hadrel could even rescue Cassie and Jay.

'What do we need to do?' I asked.

'Ssh! Let me concentrate.' Hadrel's eyes were closed. His lips moved almost imperceptibly. 'Now...'

He opened his eyes. Jay and Cassie popped into the air beside me, breathless and startled.

Cassie staggered, and I caught her arm. 'What happened?' she gasped. 'I feel terrible.'

'I just transposed you,' said Hadrel casually. She stared at him.

'You can't transpose *people*!'

'*I* can. But it usually makes them feel a bit sick. It'll wear off.'

'Who are you?' demanded Jay. 'Where are we?'

'In the hold. Hadrel's second in command here,' I said, sensing that a little flattery might help, 'but he's got the most powerful magic on the boat. He felt sorry for you, so he offered to let us go free.'

'Oh, thank you!' murmured Cassie. 'Thank you so much!' Hadrel preened himself.

'How can we get on deck without being caught?' asked Jay.

'I'll make you invisible,' said Hadrel confidently. 'No problem. But once you're over the side, you're on your own.'

'We'll be missed from the galley!'

'Not just yet. I made two simulacra to sit in your places.' Hadrel smiled at Cassie. 'Images of you. They'll be good for half an hour.'

I hoped they were more realistic than his eagle. But I was impressed with the way Hadrel was keeping his promise. 'Keep the goosehorn,' I told him. 'If you want to play it, don't use magic.'

'What? Is that *all*?'

'It's not easy, believe me,' said Jay.

Shaking his head doubtfully, Hadrel climbed the ladder. Cautiously he opened the hatch before motioning us to follow.

'Careful! It might be a trap,' Jay muttered, but when I went up the ladder I saw a group of sailors looking straight through us as though we didn't exist. All four of us drifted over the deck like a company of ghosts. Inside our shield of invisibility, I could see my companions perfectly, although everything outside had a faint rainbow shimmer. The wind flapped noisily in the sails, shrouding our footfalls.

We reached the side and looked over. I winced at the restless sea drawing its endless patterns far below. Could Cassie make it all the way down? She looked dead beat. And what about *me*? I didn't fancy that long drop into cold water, quite possibly seething with sharks. The shore was a very long way off.

'Don't worry,' said Jay, 'I'll help you.' But he looked concerned.

'Go quickly,' said Hadrel urgently. 'Quick, now.'

Cassie spoke faintly. 'I'm not leaving.'

'Cass, you'll be fine!' exhorted Jay.

She shook her head. 'I'm not going without the other galley slaves. I'm not leaving them behind.'

'Oh, *Cass*, come *on!*'

'I can't possibly free them all,' muttered Hadrel. 'I'm sticking my neck out as it is. The ship might sink, and then imagine the trouble I'd be in!'

Cassie gripped the rail. Her eyes slowly closed, and I saw a tear free itself from her lashes. It scared me.

'Cassie?' I whispered. 'Have you seen anything more?'

She shook her head. 'Still nothing.' I glanced over the rail again, at the cold sea waiting far below. I felt horribly afraid. What was the right choice? To stay, or jump?

Then I noticed another boat – a long, wide-bodied barge – ascending from the sea towards us. Hadrel stiffened.

'The supply ship! That means Syron's here. You'll have to go before he boards. I might not be able to keep the shield and the simulacra going, not if I have to hide them from him... He's too powerful. Do you hear me? You've got to jump, *now!*'

'Right,' said Jay. 'Come on, Cass, over the rail!' But Cassie shook her head determinedly.

'Not without the others.'

The supply boat was drawing up to the ship's level. It swayed gently as crates and barrels began to lift themselves from its decks and float over to ours, ready to be passed by the sailors down into the holds. Our crew couldn't keep up. Soon crates were piled high on the decks, yet I couldn't see who was unloading on the other side. Whoever it was must be using a considerable amount of magic.

'Where are their crew?' I muttered to Hadrel.

'There's only Syron. He could do it in his sleep.' There was a sulky admiration in Hadrel's voice. 'This is nothing. He's incredibly powerful. He can do anything. He made those animals in my cabin.'

'*He* made those? I thought you did.'

'No. I've tried to remake them the way they were, but it's too hard without hurting them. So I'm just looking after them because – he didn't really want them any more.'

A barrel bounced awkwardly on the deck, and burst open. A dark, gleaming pool of oil began to spread across the boards. The crewmen jumped back, swearing at the barrel and blaming each other. They seemed about to come to blows when a tall cloaked man strode over from the supply ship in a giant's leap. As he waved his hand, the oil sucked itself from the deck and stood up in a glistening, barrel-shaped column.

'Now I'll just rebuild the barrel round it,' he said, laughing, his voice as strong and compelling as his handsome face.

As the pieces of barrel flew to obey, Hadrel nudged me. 'See him? That's Syron.'

'No, it's not,' I said. 'That's my Uncle Kelver.'

Chapter 14

No sooner had I said, 'That's Uncle Kelver,' than I began to think, no, it can't be. That's a different Kelver Truso. Someone's made an image of him – I just couldn't think who or why.

So then I decided, all right, it's Uncle Kelver, but there's a reason. He's here to rescue us! But no, that didn't work. He had come as Syron, and he had been expected.

Well, then, I thought, he must be spying on the Necromancers. He's a double agent, pretending to support them while he's really uncovering their plans and plotting their defeat. Syron is his disguise.

That sounded plausible. I wanted to believe it. When I saw Lady Galera shake hands with Kelver, and embrace him, I thought how well he played his part.

'Kelver Truso,' muttered Jay. 'What's he doing here?'

Hadrel stared. 'That's *Kelver Truso*?'

'There'll be a reason,' I said.

'But that's Syron! I've known him for years!'

'So have I.'

'He must be a double agent,' said Hadrel doubtfully, 'spying on Leodwych for us. He always knows where the best pickings are to be found.' I began to feel sick. 'He's very friendly with Galera,' Hadrel went on jealously. 'He's your *uncle*? I want to know what's going on.'

I seized his arm. 'Don't tell him I'm here!' I begged, though I couldn't have said exactly why.

'I won't. But you're leaving now, anyway.'

'Not yet,' I said.

'Not without the other slaves,' said Cassie.

'*Cassie!*' hissed Jay. 'We can't help them! The guards'll catch us if we go back to the galley now!'

'I can make you invisible as far as the galley,' said Hadrel absently, 'but after that you're on your own.' As he gazed at Kelver and Lady Galera laughing, their hands on each other's shoulders, his brows drew together in distrust.

'Then I'm going back there,' said Cassie, and moved light-footed over the deck. After a few steps, she melted away into her own little pool of invisibility. Jay hesitated, then hurried after her, shaking his head as he vanished too.

Although Hadrel didn't seem to notice, I was astounded by his power. Most people had enough trouble maintaining one shield of invisibility for any length of time. Hadrel had just created two extra as an afterthought. Now, stepping behind a lifeboat, he shed his own shield in a brief fall of rainbow light.

'Don't worry, *you're* still invisible,' he muttered. 'But I need to talk to Syron. I don't understand what's going on.'

'Me neither. Can I listen?'

He nodded, took a deep breath and emerged from the lifeboat's shadow as if he'd just strolled round from the other side of the ship. Very upright and self-conscious, he walked over to Kelver. I followed just close enough to hear.

'Syron?'

Lady Galera's face tightened. Kelver said, 'Hadrel!' in a warm, happy voice: exactly the warm, happy voice he always used to greet me on entering our house. It made me want to run up and hug him the way I used to when I was small. I bit my lip.

'Good morning, Syron,' said Hadrel formally. 'I wasn't expecting you yet.'

'He came early,' said Lady Galera.

'Why wasn't I told?'

'You don't always have to be told.'

'I should know what's going on in this ship,' said Hadrel, his voice not quite steady.

'I came early,' said Kelver. 'Does it matter? My dear boy, I'm so glad to see you!' He embraced Hadrel, who stood rigid. Kelver released him with a puzzled smile. 'I thought you'd be pleased!'

'I've got a question,' said Hadrel.

'Fire away!'

'Not here. In private.'

'Well, why don't you pop down to the stateroom and I'll be along in a minute? We'll have a good chat. I've brought you a present from Leodwych.' His eyes twinkled.

'Not a goosehorn, I hope,' said Lady Galera.

'A goosehorn? No. Whatever gave you that idea?'

'Hadrel has acquired one already. You wouldn't believe the noise it made yesterday. However, I'm sure he's mastered it by now, haven't you, Hadrel? Later on, you could play for us,' suggested Lady Galera silkily.

'Wherever did you get hold of a goosehorn?' Kelver's twinkle disappeared.

'Oh, some child from Leodwych School,' said Lady Galera.

'The *school?* Why on earth have you been taking children from the school? You know that's dangerous: some of those children have powerful connections!'

'Indeed they do. But they also have *power*, Syron, they're well-trained in magic, and they were absurdly easy to take. No precautions at all. Hadrel, where is your new servant?' My heart nearly stopped, but Hadrel just said flatly,

'He's in my cabin.'

'Keep him there until I tell you. Put a binding spell on him. Run along now; I'll call you when I want you.' Her tone was dismissive.

Hadrel hesitated, then walked away, his reddening face full of frustration and doubt. I lingered for a moment, to hear Kelver say,

'Galera, I don't like you taking children from the school.'

'Why not? What's the difference? We needed the power, Syron. Why are you so bothered about the school? You don't know any children there, do you?'

'Of course not. But like I said, you could stir up trouble.'

'Trouble? What do I care about trouble down in

108

Leodwych? I've got enough trouble on board as it is,' said Lady Galera bitterly. 'That's boy's getting too big for his boots, Syron. He's impudent, disobedient, always showing off, tries to lord it over the crew—'

Kelver put a hand on hers. 'Relax. He's too young to take over for a while yet.'

'He doesn't think so! I give him another year before he tries to take over the command of the ship. And he could do it, too.'

'He won't develop his full powers for a while yet,' said Kelver reassuringly.

'He's not far off.' She gripped her hands together. 'I walk a knife edge sometimes, not sure if my magic is strong enough to hold his down. He's very powerful, Syron.'

'That's why I chose him,' said Uncle Kelver, 'to help you out.'

'I want him to go. I don't want him on board any more. You can arrange it.'

'Come now, Galera, you just said you were short of power! Who would keep your shields up if Hadrel wasn't here?'

'We'd cope.' She looked directly at Kelver. 'I want you to get rid of him.'

'I can't do that!'

'Why not? It's simple enough. Just paralyse him and throw him overboard. Or send him home, if you're senti-mental. Why the frown, Syron? I know he's your favourite discovery – but he's dangerous. I want him gone.'

'Now, Galera—'

'Perhaps we could strike a bargain.'

'A bargain? What with?'

'That goosehorn, maybe, Mr Truso?'

Kelver looked alarmed. 'Ssh! Don't call me that here. That must remain secret! Anyway, what would I want with a goosehorn?'

Lady Galera smiled, but did not answer. Kelver began to talk soothingly.

'I'll have a word with Hadrel. I think he'll listen to me. You have to make allowances, Galera: he's only a youth, and youth is headstrong. And foolish. Not like you.' Lady Galera let him kiss her hand. 'I'll go and talk to him now,' said Kelver, lingering over Lady Galera's hand before he walked away.

I dodged aside as he passed me. I knew now for sure that this was Kelver, my own Uncle Kelver, but somehow he seemed less real with every sentence he spoke. Of course he had to be friendly to Lady Galera – he was trying to win her confidence, as any double agent would.

Nevertheless, as I trailed him stealthily down the narrow gangway, still hidden in my shield of invisibility, I felt as if Kelver wore his own shield: made of layer upon layer of impenetrable shadow, so that I could no longer see who he was.

In the stateroom Hadrel was drumming his fingers on the map table. I couldn't tell if he knew I was there. He looked only at Kelver, with a fierce, intense gaze.

'Well, Hadrel,' said Uncle Kelver heartily, clapping

him on the back, 'things don't seem to be going so well between you and Lady Galera.'

'She treats me like a little kid.'

'You've got some growing up to do yet,' said Kelver gently. 'You've got plenty to learn before you even think of captaincy. There's no rush.'

'I'm tired of waiting,' said Hadrel petulantly. 'She doesn't give me a say in anything. Shield up, shield down, steer north, steer south, that's all I'm good for. I even have to provide extra power when the slaves are tired – I tell you, I feel like a slave myself! I could fly this ship with my eyes closed and one hand behind my back, and she treats me like a baby!'

Kelver was watching him closely. 'And where would you fly it to?'

Hadrel waved his arms. 'Anywhere. To see the world. To cross the ocean. To see how people live on the far islands. To see my mother.'

'Ah,' said Kelver. 'But, Hadrel, captaining a sky-ship of the Necromancers involves a lot more than little jaunts to see your mother.'

'Do you think I don't know that?' Hadrel's face flushed: I saw him flex his fingers, and waited for the sparks to fly. But then his shoulders slumped. 'Gathering riches, I know. Plundering barns and warehouses down below. Gathering slaves.'

'Gathering *power*,' Kelver corrected him.

'Such a load of bother, just to keep the ship flying,' grumbled Hadrel.

'Would you rather stay on the farm, breaking your back in the fields and living on turnips?'

'No, I wouldn't,' said Hadrel. 'It's not that I'm not grateful.'

'You don't sound very grateful.'

'It's just that – all these slaves and plunder – haven't we got enough by now? Can't we stop sailing around for a bit?'

'How would we gain such wealth without our airships?' said Kelver.

'But we don't need to keep carrying out raids for ever, do we? We've gathered more food than we can eat; we've got chests full of money...'

Kelver shook his head. 'You don't understand, do you? It's not just about gathering wealth. It's about having control: having power over those down below.' He smiled. 'We take their children, their cattle and their grain without them even knowing it. They fear us – yet they don't even know who we are! They have no idea how to stop us! They whisper our name in terror, and can do nothing.'

He put both his hands on Hadrel's shoulders and shook him gently. 'But Hadrel, that is why the captaincy is not something to be undertaken before you are ready. When I first ordered the fleet built and resurrected the ancient name of the Necromancers, even I had no idea how great our power would be over those fools down below.'

'Are they really fools?'

'Do they have airships?' retorted Kelver. 'Can they

even imagine such a thing, let alone build them? I must say, I am very proud of my airships – a great improvement on the boats the old Necromancers used to sail. Flying is so much more efficient. And the fools will never detect us!'

'They might. They have powers too,' said Hadrel.

'They don't use them properly. They're lazy. Wasting their time on tricks and toys and fancy flying carpets, while Leode's famous City turns to dust around them!' He snorted. 'They deserve all they get.'

'*You've* done all right down there,' said Hadrel sulkily. 'You're one of the Mage Council – you're Kelver Truso. Aren't you?'

Kelver's face stiffened. 'Who told you that? Galera?'

'One of the crew.'

'I thought only Galera knew.' Kelver frowned. 'Well, I would have told you, sooner or later.'

'So whose side are you on?'

'Isn't it obvious? Do you really need to ask? Yours, of course! Down there, I'm only one of twelve. Twelve dutiful old bores. It's *here*' – Kelver leaned forward – '*here* on this ship that real power is to be had. When you become captain, your authority will be total. You can do whatever you like. Even visit your mother. *But*' – he lowered his voice earnestly – 'you have to wait your turn. That could be another five years.'

'Five years!' Hadrel looked aghast.

'Maybe less. Be patient. Maybe I can help you seize power earlier.' He held up his hand as Hadrel eagerly began to speak. 'But only if you agree to do exactly as I say.'

'I can't wait five years!'

'Work with me, and it will be less.'

'It had better be less! I can't stand another six months of being bossed around by Galera!'

'Act too rashly, and she'll have you thrown off the ship.'

'She couldn't,' said Hadrel confidently.

'But I could, if you behaved stupidly.'

'I'd like to see you try!' retorted Hadrel.

'Do you mean you'd try and fight me?' Kelver looked amused.

'I might have known you'd take her side! I don't think you're on *my* side at all!'

'My dear boy—'

'I challenge you to prove whose side you're on!'

'My dear boy. You challenge me?'

'I do!' To my alarm, the stateroom began to buzz. It was becoming charged with electricity. Hadrel's face held a look of intense concentration; needles of lightning began to fizz from his fingertips. I backed cautiously away into a corner, my invisible hair standing on end.

Kelver just crossed his arms and put his head on one side, looking at Hadrel with faint amusement. The muscles of Hadrel's outstretched arms tightened, and the needles of lightning lengthened to jagged, blinding spears shooting from his fingertips. Impressive though the lightning looked, it bounced harmlessly off Kelver,

114

and ricocheted in rapid, zigzag darts around the room. I crouched down to avoid being hit.

Kelver laughed. He threw back his cloak and snapped his fingers casually. I saw Hadrel's eyes widen and his hands begin to shake. They fell to his sides, hanging there as uselessly as a puppet's wooden limbs. Hadrel looked stunned. He opened his mouth and began to speak, but his voice stopped with a croak. His eyes stared at Kelver in terror until they, too, slowly closed.

With a shock, I realised that I had just seen a duel. Only this time Hadrel had been really trying; and this time, it had been over almost before it had begun.

Kelver said in a deep, compelling voice, 'You cannot use your body or your voice against me, Hadrel. You can neither say a spell nor look one. All your spells are broken, Hadrel.'

The faint shimmer around me faded, warning me that my invisibility shield had gone. My stomach lurched as I straightened up. I wondered whether to try and sneak out unseen.

I stayed put. I wanted to hear Kelver. I was still waiting for the clue – the explanation – the moment of enlightenment when all would become clear, and I'd think: Of course! *That's* why he's doing it!

Kelver, his back to me, spoke again. 'Your spells are useless. I will restore them when I'm ready. But be careful, Hadrel, or I will take away your magic for ever.'

Hadrel made a choking noise, and Kelver laughed. 'You think I can't? Nobody else in the world could, that's true. Nobody can take away a person's magic for good. *But I've done it*. I've done it once, Hadrel, and I can do it again – to you.'

I leaned against the doorway. I couldn't have moved now if I wanted to. My legs felt weak and shaky, because I knew who Kelver was talking about. I knew whose magic he had taken.

Mine.

Chapter 15

I saw again that dream from deep in my past, of my ecstatic flight across the farmyard over the squawking hens. Not a dream: a memory. A memory of my own magic, lost forever.

'Uncle Kelver,' I said.

He spun round. I had never seen him look so shocked. As for me, I didn't know what to feel, so I decided to leave feeling for later.

'Ned!' he said hoarsely. 'Why, Ned! Whatever are you doing here? The goosehorn...great stars, is it yours? Did they capture you?'

'You took away my magic,' I said. My voice sounded thin and unreal to my own ears.

'Ned, I—' Kelver stopped and drew a deep breath. 'It was an accident.'

I considered that. It seemed unlikely. 'I don't think so.'

'Believe me, Ned, it was an accident! I was just trying out – trying to create a spell that was unique, that no one had ever done before, to remove someone's magic. I didn't expect it to work properly.'

'It worked all right,' I said. 'Why me?'

He shook his head sorrowfully. 'I didn't think it would be permanent.'

'Why me?'

He sighed and spread his hands. 'Because – well, I was angry with your mother.'

'Why?'

'For marrying your father. For staying with him in that little shack of a farmhouse, surrounded by mud. For refusing my help. I thought she could never be happy with him.'

'You loved my mother,' I said.

'I don't expect you to understand, at your age. She turned me down for your father. But she would have been happier with me.'

'It was revenge,' I said.

'It was a moment's impulse! I never imagined in a million years that it could work so well. I tried to put your magic back again. You know I tried, Ned, don't you?' appealed Kelver.

I did. I had seen his regret at being unable to help me. But I knew now that Kelver was a good actor.

'How hard did you try?' I said.

'I tried everything! But, alas, it couldn't be done. Your magic had broken so utterly that it couldn't be mended. I was more powerful than I knew.' Was there a hint of pride in his voice?

'I see,' I said. My tongue would barely move. I felt as stricken as Hadrel, whose terrified eyes were now wide open, but who still stood paralysed.

'It was an accident, a mistake!' repeated Kelver. 'It wasn't my fault. I've done all I can to make up for it, and more. You know that! Think of everything I've done for you! I sent you to the best school, I made sure your parents never went short, though your father would never accept much from me...'

'He would have accepted nothing if he'd known,' I said.

'It hasn't been that bad,' said Kelver, 'has it? You're getting a better education than any of your old friends. You'll be free of the farm and all its drudgery.' He put his hands on my shoulders reassuringly. 'I can get you a good job, Ned; I'll keep on helping you as I have always done. You've gained more than you've lost. You haven't missed much at all.'

'I wouldn't know,' I said. 'I never had the chance to find out.'

But Kelver wasn't listening. 'You've had the best of everything, no expense spared. Believe me, Ned, I felt bad about it, but I've done everything I can, including begging favours of the Mage Council.' He didn't ask me how I felt. He didn't say sorry.

'Including joining the Necromancers,' I said.

'Oh, Ned, Ned, that's just politics! That has nothing to do with you and me.'

'Including kidnapping children,' I said, 'and making slaves of my friends.'

'Ned, I would never have allowed *you* to be kidnapped if I'd known! I'll arrange for your release immediately, and fly you home myself. There's just one thing.' He smiled sadly. 'I'll have to erase your memory before I let you go.'

'No,' I said, and began to back away from his out-stretched hand. But Kelver, standing between me and the door, began to whisper soft words which made my sight blur and my mind go fuzzy. Who was this man again? What was he doing to me?

I tried to pull myself together, but I couldn't think straight. I couldn't remember where I was, or how I got here. I knew my name was Donkey. And something about a goosehorn...

A siren blared out suddenly, blowing through my head with a gale of noise. Kelver swivelled in surprise. Hadrel collapsed onto his knees, staring at me with horrified sympathy, until Kelver dragged him roughly to his feet. I had just enough presence of mind to keep the dazed look on my face, my mouth hanging open so that Kelver would not realise that his spell on me had failed.

'Move!' Kelver snapped at Hadrel. 'There's trouble on board. You'll be needed. Yes, your magic's back – just as long as you do what I say. Ned?'

I gaped blankly at nothing. Kelver studied me for a moment before he left, dragging Hadrel. I waited as long as I dared. Trouble on board? Surely that could only mean Cassie and Jay...

But when I crept out upon the sunlit deck, they were nowhere to be seen. Instead, the astonished sailors were all gazing at an extraordinary sight.

One of the lifeboats was hovering in mid-air over the ship's rail, and it was full of mermaids. Well, mer-boys too, strictly speaking. They lay casually in the lifeboat, gently flapping their tails, twirling their hair through wet fingers and singing. One of them played a harp made from the backbone of some giant fish. It was almost funny – but nobody laughed. All we could do was *listen*.

The mer-children sang the saddest, most beautiful song I had ever heard. Melodies twined in and out of each other like dying waves lamenting to the shore. I wanted to listen for ever. The whole crew was transfixed, enraptured by the sound. Even Kelver and Lady Galera stood still to listen. I remembered vaguely that I was looking for someone – but it didn't matter any more.

The lifeboat slipped over the ship's rail. As it drifted out of sight, everyone was drawn to the side after it, to listen to the dwindling song and watch the boat and its fishy passengers glide down towards the sea. Just beyond it was another lifeboat full of mermaids, that must have left minutes earlier.

Dreamily I realised that the sea was closer than before. Our ship was slowly sinking through the air. It wasn't important. All that mattered was the singing.

But the singing faded at last and was drowned out by seagulls' cries. I felt abandoned and bewildered. Uncle Kelver came suddenly to life, and roared out harshly,

'Guards! Wake up! Your slaves are escaping! You're letting the ship sink!'

Many of the crew still stood entranced, with faraway smiles. Hadrel was staring open-mouthed until Lady Galera slapped his face, and that of Rendel – equally bewitched – and hurried over to Kelver.

'Syron! We need to get those slaves back!'

'We need to stop any more escaping first,' said Kelver. He flicked an impatient hand. With a series of ear-splitting cracks, planks began to peel away from the deck like overripe banana skin, until a dark hole gaped below.

Kelver shouted into it. 'Guards down there! *Wake up! I command you!*'

I peered down into a changed, enchanted galley. It was full of mermaids. They sat on benches not of wood but of coral and shell, dabbling their tails in the tiny wavelets that sloshed around the floor.

The foremost mermaid looked up dolefully with a face as pale as the moon. She held a bone harp, and her hair glittered like starlight on water. When she opened her mouth, her song floated up and entwined us in its sad spell. The galley guards were swaying, their eyes half-closed.

I was caught again, until the sight of Jay jolted me awake. He had no tail, but was walking along a row of mer-people, muttering instructions in their ears. I couldn't see Cassie.

Uncle Kelver bellowed like a crazy bull. For an instant, the mermaids shimmered out of focus, and their song went flat, before it set itself to rights and continued as before. The mermaids and mer-boys began to float up through the broken ceiling and drift across the deck towards the third lifeboat, waving their tails serenely as if they were swimming through the air.

'Stop them!' shouted Kelver – but even Lady Galera made no answer except to murmur,

'Ah, don't stop the singing.'

'ENOUGH!' Crossing his arms, Kelver began to chant a long, stern spell. The words seemed to turn to shadows that swarmed along the deck.

The singing stopped. The mermaids who had already reached the third lifeboat became children again, dusty galley slaves. The ones still floating across the deck fell down, or staggered weakly on their new-found legs.

Kelver was screaming at the befuddled guards. 'Tie them up! Pin them down!' Nobody responded. Jay heaved himself nimbly up through the broken deck and helped the children to their feet. He gave me a cheerful grin.

'Haven't a clue what's going on, mate,' he announced too loudly. 'She made me deaf so I wouldn't get bewitched.'

'Who did?'

He nodded at the mermaid who had held the harp. The harp was now a crumbling model boat, and the girl was Cassie. She looked exhausted. Her hair was plastered to her head with sweat, not sea water.

'Had no idea she could do magic like that,' boomed Jay.

The ship pitched forward, throwing us all off our feet, and Kelver yelled again in rage. 'Guards! Wake up! The ship is *sinking*! Hold it up! Hadrel, hold the ship up, do you hear me?' He seized the limp Hadrel by the hair and shook him. 'Use your power, Hadrel!'

The ship pitched again. Everyone staggered, clinging onto rails or masts: I grabbed the nearest rope and held

123

on tight. The guards and crew began to mutter spells. Hadrel's face was tense, wincing with painful effort as the ship groaned, and steadied.

But Cassie gazed up at the lifeboat full of frightened slaves. Her lips moved, and there was a faint whisper of mermaid song. Fish tails shimmered again like silver veils over the children's legs.

Even at that whisper, the crew relaxed into smiles. The ship began to upend, so that ropes and buckets slithered and clattered along the deck.

'Stop that singing!' bawled Kelver, his face crimson and distorted with fury. Cassie took no notice.

'Stop it! I'll *make* you!' Kelver seemed to grow in height. His cloak billowed in a savage gust of wind. Fog gathered around the mast heads; thin shards of lightning crackled from them. The rope I was clutching began to quiver, and the deck vibrated.

Then Kelver began to speak, his voice so low and dark that the words were like a growl of thunder. High above us in the storm clouds came an answering rumble.

'Oh, Lord,' said Jay loudly. 'What's he saying? I can *feel* something—'

A gale struck the ship. The mainsail whumped madly, then tore right across. The taut ropes rattled on the masts. The ship lurched from side to side as though on a high sea.

Kelver laughed wildly, and pointed a triumphant finger at Cassie.

'You have no magic! It is gone!' he cried.

Above her head, with a deafening bang, the main-mast split from top to bottom. The halves began to fall apart like two felled trees.

Cassie, on her knees, tried to crawl away. I ran to drag her aside. She was white and shaking. The crew shouted and screamed, scrambling out of the way. The falling timbers thudded heavily to the deck with a deep *boom* that echoed in my head, getting louder and louder, until I clapped my hands over my ears. So did everyone else, except Kelver.

Kelver stood upright with arms spread wide, calling into the storm. I clung tight to the rail and to Cassie as the deck heaved beneath our feet and the violent wind tried to tear us away. Nearby, Hadrel was hugging a bollard for dear life.

Jay's voice yelled in my ear. 'Ned! The ship's sinking!'

I looked over the rail. The waves were closer and fiercer than before, leaping up at us like hungry dogs.

'If the ship hits the water it'll break up! We've got to jump clear!' shouted Jay. Before I could protest, he seized Cassie and pushed her over the side. She fell towards the sea, arms and legs splayed out like a starfish. I had no time to be shocked. Jay had grasped my collar and was hoisting me over the rail.

'Don't worry!' he yelled. 'I'll help you fly down.'

'Wait!' I turned to Hadrel, shouting, 'Hadrel, jump clear—' Then I was overboard, and falling alongside Jay.

Within a second, the wind had ripped me from his grasp. I was tumbling headlong towards the sea, which charged up to meet me, surly and snarling, showing its white teeth. I waited for Jay to slow me down – but it didn't happen. There was no time to do anything but take a last frantic gulp of air before the sea hit me like a wallop from a giant boxing glove.

Chapter 16

I sank a long way. The sea pressed on me, cold and heavy, trying to hold me under. I didn't know which way was up until I opened my eyes and saw a pale green glimmer ahead. I fought my way towards it, hitting the surface just before my lungs gave up.

Gasping thankfully, I trod water amongst the choppy waves. Jay and Cassie surfaced nearby, spluttering. Next thing I knew, the lifeboat had plunged down next to us and swamped us with its splash, surrounded by the smaller splashes of children who had fallen out of it on the way down. Mermaids no longer, they flailed in the water until we helped them reach the lifeboat's side. Cassie clung to it with her eyes closed.

Then the children began to shriek and point. Above us, the huge bulk of the Necromancers' ship was foundering, tipping onto its prow. Slowly at first, then with gathering speed, it fell from the sky.

Everyone began kicking as hard as they could to steer the lifeboat out of the ship's path. Ten seconds passed – eleven – twelve – and then I heard behind me a long, resounding crash, as if the ship had hit a solid wall instead of water.

A massive wave lifted me right up and dunked me. When I surfaced again, the ship's stern was sticking out of the water while the waves pounced on it, foaming angrily, tearing at it like a pack of snarling wolves until it disappeared beneath their attack.

All around us fell yelling sailors, scraps of sail and ropes and buckets and benches, plopping into the water and disappearing from sight. Then they all started to come up again: men and boxes and barrels and spars of wood bobbed to the surface amidst huge bubbles of air, as if the sea were boiling.

Jay and I draped our arms across a drifting plank and hung on as huge waves full of flotsam rocked past us. We were too stunned to talk.

'We're a long way from land,' croaked Jay at last. I couldn't see any land at all. But I knew where it was – to the west, away from the sun, which was beginning to shine again. The storm clouds thinned and were rapidly blown away. The gigantic swell created by the foundering ship became gentler. Slowly the sea calmed.

The children clambered into the lifeboat. When some of the sailors climbed in too, the children didn't try to stop them. They all sat bedraggled and shivering together.

The guards, however, had disappeared. I shuddered as I thought of their chain mail pulling them down as inexorably as an anchor to the sea bed. Then I thought, no, they'll have used magic to free themselves. No problem! I expect they're floating around in the sky.

I looked up at a sky empty but for clouds, and was puzzled. Why hadn't the crew flown themselves to safety? Why was everyone floundering so desperately in the sea instead of floating above it, or magicking themselves nice little boats? I saw Hadrel trying unsuccessfully to pull himself onto a barrel which kept rolling away.

'Hadrel!' I yelled. 'Why don't you use magic?'

'Can't,' he gasped, spitting out a mouthful of water, and added something that sounded like, 'Not there,' before he sank again. I swam over to him, grabbed his collar and yanked him towards a floating cabin door. Crawling onto it, Hadrel lay there exhausted with the water washing over his legs.

Luckily the sea was warm, as seas go, and calm now that the storm had passed. All the same, I didn't fancy staying in the water for long. I wondered how far we were from shore. As a piece of the ship's prow bobbed past, I scrambled up it as high as I could manage and gazed round the horizon. No land anywhere – or maybe I just wasn't high enough to see it.

I scanned the floating wreckage for survivors. There was no sign of Lady Galera. And Uncle Kelver? Did I want to find him or not? When at last I glimpsed him clinging to the split mainmast, I felt sorry. Then I felt glad. Then I felt sorry again, and sorry that I felt sorry.

I swam back to the lifeboat. It was too low in the water.

'Oy!' I shouted, and the sailors turned doleful faces towards me. They were so limp and soggy and hopeless that I felt quite impatient. 'Get a grip!' I told them. 'You look like a pile of wet dishrags! There's enough wood and rope floating around here to make a dozen rafts.

Why don't you collect them and start lashing them together?'

One of them mumbled a reply.

'What's that?'

'We can't,' he repeated dismally. 'We've got no magic. We can't do it.'

'What's happened to your magic?' He shrugged, shoulders slumping. 'Well, you're *sailors*, aren't you? You can tie knots, can't you?' They nodded dumbly. 'And swim?'

They shook their heads. So Jay and I swam round collecting planks and steering them to the lifeboat. There was plenty of rope floating around, and within half an hour some of the sailors had made a raft big enough to sit on while they lashed barrels to the sides for extra buoyancy. By the time they'd finished they weren't looking quite so helpless. They even fixed up a sail. I got them to fix one in the lifeboat too.

With the sailors on the raft, there was room in the lifeboat for the rest of us. Hadrel sat hunched and dripping, not looking at his former slaves. I climbed in thankfully, for I was getting very cold, and asked the biggest children, who had the oars, to row over to Kelver.

Kelver was still clinging to the mainmast. We dragged him into the lifeboat, his teeth chattering, his eyes barely open. He seemed not to know what was happening or where he was.

'Be all right in this sun,' said Jay. 'He just needs to warm up.'

130

'Galera,' murmured Hadrel. 'The officers. The animals. Syron, you drowned all the animals!' His face twisted. He shook Kelver until I pulled him away.

'What's that over there?' said Jay, pointing at something glinting in the water. It was the goosehorn, caught up in a tangle of ropes. I leaned over to retrieve it. After pouring out the sea water, I put it to my lips to blow out the last drops.

'Don't!' cried Jay, clapping his hands over his ears. 'It hurts now Cassie's cured my deafness!'

'Not on purpose,' said Cassie. 'The spell just broke. My magic's gone. I don't know where it is any more.' She sounded blank.

'Mine too,' said Jay, 'but it'll come back in a bit, I expect.'

'It had better,' muttered Hadrel. 'It *has* to.' He put his head in his hands.

'Has everyone's magic gone?' I asked, and looked around the boat at the damp, nodding heads.

'I bet *his* hasn't.' Jay gestured at the shivering Kelver. 'That was some spell, wasn't it? Never seen anything like it! We must have been too close to Cassie when he took away her magic, so it worked on us too. The spell might wear off, though. I'd make him take it off now if he was properly conscious.'

He scanned the sea. The other two lifeboats were bobbing in the distance, heading west. 'We'd better make for shore. Shall I row?'

We took turns at rowing. Each of the long oars needed

131

two people to pull it. Not everyone was strong enough, and some of the kids got sea-sick and had to lie down in the bottom of the boat. We made slow progress until we met a breeze that filled our little sail. Then we sat back in relief, drinking from a barrel of fresh water that had survived its fall unbroken. The sailors on the raft were drifting out of sight, heading north.

Cassie and Hadrel took turns at the rudder. Kelver did nothing. Just sat there like a stunned man. At last a horizon that wasn't sea edged into sight through the spray. We crept towards it at a sea-snail's pace. It was well into the afternoon before the coast was clearly visible.

'That's the Garinth light-tower!' cried Jay excitedly. 'I'm sure of it!' The light-tower was a famous landmark, only a dozen miles up the coast from our old swimming bay.

'The light's out,' remarked Cassie.

'That doesn't matter. We'll make land well before dark.'

'I hope,' I said. The wind had pushed us close to shore, but now it veered the wrong way and we had to furl the sail again. None of us could row for very long; the boat was too heavy, and we were too tired.

I looked over at Kelver. He was the only adult on board – if he would take a turn, it would help a lot. It was the least he could do. Although his eyes were closed, I didn't think he was asleep. I wriggled over a couple of sea-sick children to reach him.

'Uncle Kelver!' I shook him until he opened his eyes.

'Can you row? We need you to row, or you could magic the oars if you're too tired.'

He didn't look at me. His eyes, dull and sunken, stared at nothing.

'Kelver! Wake up! What was that spell? What did you *do*?'

His voice was hardly more than a breath. 'Took the girl's magic away.'

'You took *everyone's* magic away!' I said. 'How long are the effects going to last? Can't you speed it up? Then we won't need to row to shore.' Kelver just kept shaking his head feebly. I felt exasperated. 'All right, then, conjure us a couple of extra oars! Even that would help!'

He kept shaking his head. My skin began to crawl.

'Why not, Kelver?'

'I can't,' he muttered. 'It's all gone. My magic, it's all gone.'

'Well, you dopey great galoot,' I said. There were a few other names I wanted to call him, but I had more important things to do. As we neared the shore the sea was growing choppy, the currents crossing each other in clashing waves that rocked the boat and made the sea-sick children groan. I crawled back to the prow to guide the rowers in towards the safest-looking piece of coastline.

Eventually we pulled into a wide bay backed by low cliffs, about a mile from the light-tower. I jumped out and swam ahead to check for hidden rocks that might hole us. When it was shallow enough, everyone else climbed out and hauled the boat up onto the shingle. Only Kelver still lay inside it.

I was too tired to care. I knelt on the shingle at the sea's edge and let my hands sink in gratefully amongst the cool stones. The sea hissed gently behind me, friendly and playful, and I whispered thanks to it for letting us come safely back to land.

All along the beach, weary children slumped like basking seals. Cassie sprawled on her back to drink in the last of the sun's warmth.

'If I had my magic, I'd make a fire,' she said.

Hadrel collapsed beside me. 'I'm shattered. I don't think I can walk. I've got no strength.'

'It'll come back,' said Jay, 'and so will our magic.' But he sounded less certain. 'How long has this spell lasted now? Four hours, is it?'

'More like six,' I said.

There was a shout. Three heads were peering over the top of the low cliff above us. Two girls and a boy, younger than me, stared down open-mouthed.

'Are you shipwrecked?' cried one of the girls.

'Looks like it,' I said.

'There's two more of them boats landed in the next bay! We saw them!'

'That's good. Where's the best way up these cliffs?'

'The path's over there,' said the other girl, pointing, 'but it's a bit tricky. Can't you fly?'

'Nope.'

'Magic yourself some steps?' she suggested.

'Can't do that either,' I said. 'Can you do it for us?' She shook her head.

'Why not?' asked Jay.

'Don't know. Just can't.' The three heads disappeared. Cassie began to laugh.

'What's so funny?' I asked.

'They can't,' said Cassie. 'Oh, Ned! I was so sure we were going to die on that ship. All I could foresee was a huge black emptiness, and I was convinced that meant death.' She laughed again, in happy disbelief. 'But it's not the end of everything at all! It's only my foresight that's ended! It's only my magic! We've got a whole new future that I just couldn't see!'

'You mean your magic's not coming back?' asked Jay.

'No. It's gone forever!'

'How can it?' said Jay, bewildered. 'Not even Kelver could do *that*. And what about the rest of us?'

'*No!*' Hadrel was white and horror-stricken. 'A future without magic? We'll never survive! I'd rather *die*!'

Chapter 17

I remember how I stood bedraggled on that beach, listening to the endless quiet whisper of the waves, and feeling as if time had stopped. As if the world had stopped, and then restarted differently. We had stepped out of the sea into a new world, a world washed clean of magic.

Not everyone believed it straight away. When Hadrel jumped back into the lifeboat to pummel the unresisting Kelver, Jay dragged him off, saying soothingly,

'No, no, it's all right! No spell lasts for ever. Your magic will come back.'

'What if it doesn't?' cried Hadrel, his face wet with sea water and tears. 'Magic's all I've got!' Several of the younger children caught his grief and started crying too. Jay looked anxious. Only Cassie was smiling, at ease as I'd never seen her.

'I hope mine never comes back,' she said. 'My fore-sight poisoned my life. Some of the other stuff was fun, but it went wrong as often as it went right. It's not trustworthy, magic. Now then.' She put her hands on her hips. 'What are we going to do with this lot? Everyone's wet and cold and it's only an hour or so till sunset.'

We rounded up the children – there were twenty-five of them – and tried to stop them weeping. Although a few looked older than us, they were all so weakened by

136

their imprisonment and shattered by the loss of their magic that they seemed unable to think for themselves. I promised that if they would just climb the cliff, we'd find food and warmth for them by nightfall. I had no idea where.

We hauled Kelver out of the boat. I had to support him, since he seemed unable or unwilling to walk on his own. Hadrel carried the goosehorn.

Once we had struggled up the rough steps in the rockface, and crossed a couple of barley fields, we came to a farmhouse where an old man was picking straw-berries in the evening sun. Straightening up, he stared at our weary troop with less interest than I would have expected.

I began to explain. 'We've been shipwrecked off the beach back there. We just wondered if you might have an empty barn or somewhere we could...'

I got no further. The farmer threw down his basket and cursed, loud and long. After a moment, though, I realised that he wasn't cursing us.

'...if I *had* a barn which still had a danged roof on it, which I mended with a new sealing charm only last week, and look at the danged thing now! And the danged strawberries are all set to rot in the fields, because the danged picking spell broke and there's no danged way I can get it to work again...'

'We can pick your strawberries for you,' I said, 'if you can give us some food in return. We don't mind sleeping in a barn with no roof.'

So that was what we did. With all of us helping, his whole crop was picked by nightfall. We ate more strawberries than we put in the baskets – they tasted magic, if you like – but the farmer didn't seem to mind. He gave us a heap of loaves that he grumpily told us would go stale otherwise, since none of his danged preserving spells were working, as well as a pair of dead chickens that the barn roof had fallen onto. We borrowed a flame and made a fire of bits of roof to roast the chickens, and ate charred meat and bread by the glowing embers in the dark.

Then we all huddled down in the roofless barn to sleep. With hay packed around us, it was warm enough, but I couldn't do more than doze. I was thinking about Kelver.

He lay in the hay next to me, hardly breathing. On the trek here, he'd leaned heavily on my arm until I felt lopsided. He hadn't spoken. He'd neither picked strawberries, nor eaten any bread and chicken. He just sat propped against the wall, limp as a rag doll.

Now I didn't know what to say to him. I felt tears prickle at my eyes, and was glad it was dark, though none of the children would have thought it odd of me to cry. But unlike them, I wasn't grieving for my lost magic, but for my lost uncle.

When we set off early the next day, he hung heavily on my arm again.

'Are you hurt?' I asked. 'Are you sick?' He shook his head slowly.

'I could take him for a bit,' offered Jay.

'No,' I said. 'He's my responsibility.'

'Mine too,' said Hadrel. 'I'll take a turn.' There were shadows under his tired eyes, and I guessed he hadn't slept much either. He handed me the goosehorn, and took Kelver's arm. 'Syron?' he said quietly. 'Syron? Are you all right?' There was no answer.

Soon after midday we came to the outskirts of Leodwych. We'd lost a few children, who had taken other roads to their own homes, but the rest of the former slaves plodded wearily through the town with us. The streets were almost deserted: we saw only a few quiet huddles of people, and a woman running in tears.

The market squares were empty. Half the Guildhall had tumbled down where magic rather than mortar had held its bricks together. Kelver's new bridge was a pile of rubble damming the river. I steered Kelver aside so that he wouldn't see it. I couldn't tell if he noticed or not. He didn't seem to notice anything.

Luckily Leode's old bridge still stood unchanged. Hadrel paused halfway across, looking bemused.

'It's a bigger place than I realised,' he said. 'I thought Leodwych was just a shanty town. You know, pigs in the streets, beggars in rags everywhere. That's what *he* told me.' He nodded at Kelver. 'He said that's why they were no worse off as slaves.'

Kelver didn't seem to hear. His eyes were blank. As we moved on, the children's heads twisting round at each new sight, Kelver never looked up, not even when we crossed the Plaza. Just two days ago it had been full

139

of crowds and candyfloss: now it was deserted. Leode's statue gazed serenely over the dead fountains.

We walked on to the school. Unwinged sheep grazed contentedly on the flyball pitch, but the buildings were in disarray. The bell tower had collapsed completely. Doors had fallen off their hinges, and windows out of their frames. Pupils sat on the crumbling steps or clumped in the corridors, talking in subdued voices. Marta, Bruno and the others jumped up and ran to meet us.

'Where've you been?' cried Marta. 'It's been terrible here! You wouldn't believe what's happened!'

'The whole school started to fall down,' burst in Hanni, 'we thought it was an earthquake—'

'Wragg's gone mental,' said Gowan with satisfaction.

Bruno gave Jay a bear hug before retreating in grinning embarrassment. 'Good to see you, man,' he said, and even clapped me on the shoulder. 'We got worried about you. Thought you'd been taken by the Necromancers. It's been weird here since yesterday.'

'We know. It's weird everywhere,' said Jay.

'Would you believe that none of us can do any magic?'

'Oh yes,' I said. 'I believe it.'

Marta was staring at Hadrel and Kelver. 'Isn't that Kelver Truso? Has he come to put things right? Who's that boy with him?'

Hadrel opened and closed his mouth and said nothing.

'He was a slave on the Necromancers' ship,' I said. 'You were right, they did capture us, but we escaped.

We'll tell you later. Right now we need to find Mr Wragg. Where is he?'

'In his room. But he's gone crazy,' Bruno warned us. 'Keeps shouting and howling.'

We crept into Mr Wragg's office to find him crouched at his desk, muttering. He was surrounded by upturned crucibles, broken jars, and tumbled books. His fist crashed onto his desk, making everything on it bounce. 'Why won't you work?' he shouted.

'Mr Wragg?'

'Get out of here, boy!' Then he noticed Kelver. His expression changed as he leapt to his feet. 'Mr Truso? Are you all right? What have these boys done to you?'

'*We've* done nothing to *him*,' said Jay angrily, 'apart from save his life when he didn't deserve it!'

Mr Wragg ignored him to appeal to Kelver. 'Mr Truso! I need your help! I'm in trouble here! My power,' he said in anguish, 'my power, it's all gone!'

Kelver was mute. I said, 'He can't help right now. We need to call the Mage Council together. Maybe they can do something. Can you arrange a meeting?'

He stared at me wildly. 'Don't be stupid, boy. Meet for *you*? Anyway, how am I supposed to summon them now?'

'Very easily,' said an acerbic voice. 'Send out foot-messengers. An excellent idea.' Miss Lithgoe had entered behind us. There were anxious creases between her eyes, but now she smiled. 'I'm glad you made it safely home. We'll summon the Council to meet here, at the school.'

That evening the Mage Council gathered in Mr Wragg's classroom, a bunch of bewildered old people perched on battered school chairs, lit by the smoky flicker of candlelight rather than the magical brilliance of lamps. Kelver must have been the youngest of them: yet now, slumped in a chair next to Hadrel, he looked like the oldest.

Miss Lithgoe had ordered one child from every class to attend, but the slaves had been taken away to be fed and comforted. Since Mr Wragg had locked himself in his room with his spell books, refusing to come out, Miss Lithgoe chaired the meeting herself.

'I confess,' said the spidery old lady, Dorea, 'I am quite bewildered by the turn events have taken. I have no idea what can have happened to my magic. None of us have any idea.'

'It was nothing to do with any of us,' added Harlo.

'Yes, it was,' I said, looking at Kelver. 'Are you going to tell them?'

He was silent, so I began to tell the tale, starting with the concert. Jay and Cassie took a turn, and Hadrel mumbled his part, downcast and overawed, but truthfully describing both the duels he had lost – to me and to Kelver.

Kelver said nothing at all. To every question that was put to him, he shook his head slowly, like an empty man: a hollow man with nothing inside him.

'Kelver took away our magic?' asked Harlo in disbelief.

'He only meant to take Cassie's magic,' I said, 'as he once took mine. Only he got the spell wrong, or it got itself wrong, and worked on everyone.'

'Until it wears off,' Jay added, 'or he revokes it.'

'But Kelver has no magic either,' said Harlo, bewildered. 'How can he undo his own spell?'

'Somewhere in the country there must still be magic,' Dorea answered briskly. 'It can't *all* have gone. If we send out word to bid all those with magic to come here to Leodwych—'

'Yes! That's the answer.' The Mages brightened up. 'We need magic to restore our magic. It's just a matter of finding it.'

'And meanwhile...?' enquired Miss Lithgoe.

'Meanwhile, we wait,' said Harlo confidently. 'We'll study Leode's *Book of the City*, and other works of magic lore, to see what wisdom they can offer us.' All the Mages got up and began to shuffle out, chatting more cheerfully now they had decided on a course of action.

Once they had left, Miss Lithgoe shook her head. 'We might wait a long time for something to happen.'

'I don't think anything *will* happen,' said Cassie. 'I don't think there is any magic left, anywhere. Is there, Mr Truso?'

'I don't know,' Kelver muttered. 'How would I know? There's none left for me.'

Miss Lithgoe gave him a sharp glance. 'We will not try to pretend to the pupils that things are normal.

143

However, we need to adapt as best as we can.' She put her hands together thoughtfully. 'School will resume tomorrow in all classrooms that are fit to be used. We will stick to the timetable; but extra lessons will be added in place of the magic classes.'

'What lessons?' said Jay, looking depressed.

'Lessons in learning to do without magic,' said Miss Lithgoe. 'I think we may all need to learn to do without, and the wisest of us will be those who learn fastest.'

She looked directly at me. 'And the best person – the only person – who can teach us *that*, is Ned.'

Chapter 18

Kelver sits in his little room, now, and seldom ventures out. I've asked him to come and talk to classes, or to see how the town is being rebuilt, or go for a walk down to the sea; but he won't. The mention of the sea made him wince. Mostly, he doesn't even look out of the window.

My father came over to the school for a week. He gave us some useful lessons on how to make things of wood and iron and rope without magic: how to use drills and saws and glue. He seemed totally unaffected by his loss – according to him, the farm was the same as ever, though one of the cows was lame. At the end of the week, he said,

'I expect you'll be staying on here now, after all.'

'I can't, after this term. We haven't paid the fees.'

My father smiled dryly. 'I don't think that'll matter. It'd be good if you came home for a bit, though, to see your mam. She misses you.'

'I know. I miss her too, and you, and the dogs. I even miss Ellen.' My father laughed. 'I will come home,' I promised. 'But I don't think I can stay long; there's too much to do here. Do you think Miss Plumbly would come and help us out? Most of the teachers are pretty useless without magic.'

'She's got enough to do back home, with everyone wanting lessons in reading and writing.'

I sighed. 'That's what I'm teaching here.' Cassie and Miss Lithgoe were helping me – though even they admitted, shamefacedly, that they couldn't read as well as they'd like. Not enough practice.

Miss Lithgoe and Mr Fellows were the only teachers who were any good without magic. Some of the teachers left: Miss Ibbs decided to become a pupil and sit in, tearfully, on the lessons, which was a bit embarrassing. Before long, other adults from the town joined her, until the classes were twice the size they used to be. Some people offered, like my father, to give practical lessons on building, plumbing and medicine, skills that were sorely needed. The school became busy and purposeful.

A few masons and carpenters were found with enough skills to start rebuilding the school. Bruno spent his spare time helping them, and looked happier than he ever had before. He even started work on the clock for the new clock tower. It's at Mrs Bolsher's now, taking up a whole bunk.

Hadrel moved in at Mrs Bolsher's too; luckily her house was intact, and she'd always cooked without magic. Hadrel began helping Mr Fellows teach maths, which he had a natural knack for, and I didn't.

'I never used magic for maths,' he said. 'It was more interesting without.' Miss Lithgoe decided, and Hadrel agreed, that he should stay at the school for now, along with a few ex-slaves who were too far from home to get back easily. Transport was difficult.

Bridges were broken, carriages kept losing their wheels; the entire new fishing fleet sank on its first magic-free trip out from the harbour. Luckily the fishermen were rescued.

'In due course,' Miss Lithgoe said to Hadrel, 'when things are more reliable, you can go and find your home.'

'I hope that doesn't take too long,' said Hadrel wistfully. But in the meantime, since no one knew he was a Necromancer except me and Jay and Cassie – and we weren't telling – he soon began to make friends and fitted in surprisingly well. He had lost his arrogance along with his magic. 'Got nothing to boast about now, have I?' he says these days. 'Except maths.'

Quite apart from reading and writing and building and cookery, there was a lot to learn – and unlearn. There were loads of accidents as people forgot they couldn't do magic and stepped out of windows or tried to fly. Some children barely knew how to walk upstairs. Not that we had many stairs to start with. Mr Wragg ordered a ladder to be built to the library, and skipped up it like a demented monkey to throw down armfuls of books.

'Start reading, boy!' he'd bellow. So, in the evenings, I started reading books on magic aloud to him, while he'd periodically howl in rage and frustration and rip a book from my hands to hurl it to the floor.

'Useless! All useless!' he cried. After a while I

stopped reading to him. It wasn't doing him any good.

I retrieved Leode's *Book of the City* from his fireplace, though, and sneaked it off to Mrs Bolsher's to read right through myself, lying on my bed. I was looking for useful tips on how Leode had first built the town. It struck me that Leode, the First Mage, didn't seem to use much magic. His workmen had used their hands, not magic, to do his great building works.

And stranger still – in the whole *Book of the City*, Leode made no mention of anything magical happening, at all, ever, before he started his own great works.

I rolled over and stared at the ceiling, wondering about the First Mage. What if he really *was* the first? – the very first human to have magic, a power so great that he was able to cast a spell to endow everyone else with magic too? But maybe he didn't trust magic or use it much to start with: he relied on the workmen's hands, not spells, when he built his city.

And the goosehorn. I looked over at my goosehorn, propped up in the corner. It was just a piece of brass now, no longer a writhing serpent. It was hoarse since its dousing in sea water, and I was no longer the school's best player. Anyone could play the goosehorn, provided they practised enough. Jay, who had battled with the goosehorn for three years, suddenly found himself a brilliant player, and was teaching Hadrel. I rather missed watching its wrestling matches with Jay.

Why had Leode invented the goosehorn, an instrument that sounded worse the more magic you used

148

on it? I think I know the answer. He wanted to remind people that magic could not do everything.

Kelver thought it could. I watch Kelver nowadays, rocking quietly in his chair, looking at nothing. He was the greatest Mage, people said, since Leode – the first man whose powers rivalled Leode's own. Leode gave the world magic. Kelver took it all away, with a single, selfish, cruel spell. So much easier to break than make.

But Kelver has broken himself, as well, and I don't know if he can be mended. I don't feel so bitter about him now. He doesn't have much of a life.

Hadrel still cares about Kelver. He visits him and tries to talk to him, and though he doesn't complain, I know he gets upset when Kelver just ignores him. I know it because I feel the same way. But I've decided now that Kelver never really cared for me – at least, not as much as he did for himself. It wasn't me he liked: it was the power he had over me. That was all he cared about. It hurts.

I try to feel sorry for Kelver. Sometimes I get annoyed that he won't even attempt to do things. I tell him that although he's lost his power, there's still plenty he can do. I don't think he listens. I think he's waiting for his magic to return. He can't face a future without it.

But we're all facing that future. After Leode first invented magic, I guess that people got so used to it that they forgot things hadn't always been that way. Maybe in the future – the new, strange future that even Cassie can't foresee – maybe people will forget again. They'll forget we once had magic powers, and think that wizards and spells and flying carpets are just fairy stories.

Then someone else will come along, another Leode, a new First Mage, and start it off again: the whole magic cycle.

Until then, we're all minus magic.